More Praise fo

"Donovan Montgomery is a badass forensic psychiatrist with a versatile arsenal of weapons, both mental and physical. She's going to need all of them, because her testimony in the trial of a white supremacist has put a target on her back. I read *Make It Right* in one sitting, impelled through the fast-moving plot by the dire circumstances and Donovan's bad-assery and sense of mystery. A gripping tale with more than one mystery at its core."

—Maya Kaathryn Bohnhoff, *New York Times* best-selling author of *The Antiquities Hunter*

"Donovan Montgomery is part Kinsey Millhone, part Hannibal Lecter— and all brilliant. A malevolent, intricate tale of murder and madness."

—David Niall Wilson, *USA Today* best-selling author of *Deep Blue* and *This Is My Blood*

"Jackson's debut novel blends elements of suspense and legal drama to create an action-packed, fast-paced crime thriller. Esteemed forensic psychiatrist Donovan Montgomery is preparing to give expert testimony at the murder trial of neo-Nazi Mason Ghetz, when a mass shooting claims the life of investigator Maurice Brown. Montgomery is caught in the crossfire. When the smoke clears, she gives shocking testimony for the prosecution, but to everyone's surprise, Ghetz is cleared of all charges. With Ghetz on the loose and her reputation tainted, Montgomery is determined to discover the truth and get justice by any means necessary. As readers enter Montgomery's world, they quickly realize the good doctor isn't exactly what she appears, a revelation that comes early and takes some suspense away from the plot. However, as the true nature of Montgomery's work unfolds, crime junkies and thrill seekers will enjoy the twists and turns she experiences in search of the truth. Racial and political conflict increase already high tension as Montgomery, who is black, takes on high-ranking members of the Aryan Brotherhood and other white supremacist organizations. The racial and homophobic dialogue used can be jarring at times, but it adds to the story's darkness and stakes. Jackson excels at weaving aspects of Montgomery's life, backstory, and relationships with minor characters into the narrative. The chemistry between Montgomery and sometimes love interest Tristan Liaquat sizzles and showcases a different side of the otherwise formidable femme fatale. The author's medical experience is evident throughout the story, but shines in the character Alfredo Ramos, Cook County medical examiner and "one of the few people [Montgomery] considered to be a friend." Despite there being no doubt of Ghetz's guilt or the lengths Montgomery will go to "make it right," readers will be guessing until the end. **Takeaway:** Fans of true crime and courtroom legal dramas will delight in this tale of vigilante justice. **Great for fans of:** Walter Mosley, Kathy Reichs's Temperance Brennan series."

—*Publishers Weekly*

"Chicago-based forensic psychiatrist Donovan Montgomery is an African American woman whose area of expertise has helped solve major crimes: her testimony is sought in trials; her books about the psychopathology of murderers, as well as her ability to build their profiles, are read and followed by law enforcement professionals. But Donovan is also transforming. She is turning into something she has no control over: a vigilante, a killer who will balance the books whenever she sees there's a catastrophic failure in the justice system. *Make It Right* is thoroughly absorbing because Donovan's mental struggles with good and evil provide no clear black and white definitions of perps and good people, but skates on the thin grey line between them. When trapped in a mass shooting that kills innocent peers and places her own life in jeopardy, Donovan's hardwiring allows her to act decisively and rationally both during the crisis and in its aftermath: 'Donovan remained collected and discerning in sharing her opinions about shooter versus shooters, the logical vantage point (or points) of the attack, and possible motivation. She was no one's fool and could not be bullied by the press for statements, no matter how respectful and professional the interrogation.' Her life isn't just about justice and the redemption of criminals or murderers, however. Undercurrents of racism and patriotism pervade the story, and it's Donovan's confrontations, decisions, and how she navigates the legal, political, and criminal justice bureaucracies that are fascinating to watch as she struggles personally to right obvious wrongs and tackle injustice. These themes are actually as much at the heart of the story as is Donovan's own psychological metamorphosis; the plot's twists and turns ultimately lead the psychiatrist to justify the very actions she herself commits—actions that she would condemn (and treat) in others. There are many intriguing subplots and engaging elements throughout the thriller, including a kinky relationship with lover Tom Karp (and his richly described opulent lifestyle), along with her discovery of his sketchy extracurricular activities (and her determination to personally right this wrong, too). Donovan is a strong, likeable, achievement-oriented woman whose values and viewpoints are constantly tested. As the plot evolves, readers, too, may find their own ideals, concepts of justice, and moral insights put on trial. After all, when the justice system is perceived to be falling apart, who can step up to glue it back together? This book provides an answer: Donovan Montgomery, that's who. Author Dr. Willie Mae Jackson provides a gripping, realistic story that goes far beyond the usual mystery or psychological thriller. While riddles, suspense, and mind games flavor the overall tale, it's the social issues that permeate both Donovan's life and the plot. The end result is a powerful novel that will resonate especially well with readers who like their books authentic, exciting, unpredictable, and imbued with a respectful nod to the challenges we face every day."

—Midwest Book Review

"This smart, tight debut novel by Willie Mae Jackson, *Make It Right*, has been brilliantly built as both a high-speed page-turner and a first-rate Netflix or Amazon Prime movie. Some familiar (and topical) elements are expertly connected in an exciting suspenseful mystery-thriller: Neo-Nazis, white supremacists, political corruption, a mass shooting event, injustice to be fought, and a heroine who is not strictly who she first appears to be. I love books and movies with a strong female lead, and *Make It Right* certainly doesn't disappoint—that Dr. Donovan Montgomery is also African American adds a layer of uniqueness to the story. Jackson weaves an intriguing plot that gallops along, and her intimate, professional knowledge of the machinations of the psychopathic mind lends a spell-binding authenticity to the proceedings. Jackson has an uncanny knack for putting you right inside the psycho's head, whether you want to be there or not. *Make It Right* is a terrific read for lovers of high-octane thrillers with intelligence—and the elements of white power extremism and domestic terrorism are as timely as they could possibly be. Highly recommended."

—James H. Longmore, author of the psychological thrillers
Flanagan, Tenebrion, and *Pede*

"Is this a sensational novel about vigilante justice and setting the karmic record straight or a voyeuristic look at a Sherlock-smart serial killer in a skirt who really enjoys her work? That's going to be for the reader to decide. It's also one of the many reasons you are not going to be able to put down this page-turner. Pitting a celebrated African American doctor against a neo-Nazi bad guy with a backstory lurid enough to compete with today's headlines, *Make It Right* will have you wondering if you're reading fiction or something gleaned from the six-o'clock news. In this drum-tight, uber-twisty thriller, Willie Mae Jackson has given us the scariest, sexiest, most complicated heroine in Doctor Donovan Montgomery: black, brilliant, movie star-gorgeous, and a forensic psychiatrist—just like the author. With boxer Jackie Brown's moves and Dexter's Yankee ingenuity, the spellbinding Donovan leans into her eccentricities, the most pronounced of which is a hyper-sense of order and fetish-like fixation on 'making things right.' Sometimes she works within the law to accomplish this; sometimes she takes matters into her own hands. When the latter is employed, she is the wickedest badass you never want to meet. The only people who know that side of the doctor are dead. Set in present-day Chicago, the author has integrated its nooks and crannies, shimmer and gloom in such a realistic, visceral fashion that the city itself becomes another major character in a story filled with memorable souls. The plot is fresh, the dialogue is snappy, and the characters are as flawed and jagged as a jailhouse shiv. From the first page to the last, I can't remember being this riveted to a book."

—Lee Adams, author of *5th and Vanguard* and *Nighthawks* (Julie Page Mystery Series)

"For fans of Taylor Stevens's Vanessa Michael Munroe novels (*The Informationist*), Willie Mae Jackson has created another outstanding female protagonist who is beautifully flawed, incredibly intelligent, and more than willing to step outside of the law without concern or care for conscience or consequence in order to snare her man—or woman. *Make It Right* delivers action, intrigue, ruthless killers (on both sides of the law), and peril as our heroine (a criminal psychiatrist; the author is an actual forensic psychiatrist) investigates a gross miscarriage of justice then winds up unraveling a conspiracy right out of today's headlines. The characters are nicely twisted (especially Dr. Donovan) and entirely believable, the storyline is engrossing, and it leaves you wondering if the doctor's job dealing with the criminally deranged made her the way she is, or did she choose the career because her own mind can empathize? Maybe a very welcome and anticipated sequel will answer that question."

—Anneliese Khalil, author of *Ascension*

"Move over Coffy, Proud Mary, Jackie Brown, Cleopatra Jones, and Foxy Brown. You can now add to that elite list an absolutely unique badass black woman for a new generation: the ridiculously smart, wickedly insightful, indomitably brave Dr. Donovan Montgomery. She's a renowned criminal psychiatrist and expert witness who is Krav Maga trained, as sexy as all hell, and has a brutal, ruthless streak that is eerily, cinematically magnetic. Far removed from Thomas Harris's more vulnerable and easily manipulated Clarice Starling (*Silence of the Lambs*), Donovan is experienced and world-weary enough to kick ass and leave behind her an impressive body count in order to bring justice to the streets of Chicago. Author Willie Mae Jackson's style is crisp, uncluttered, and has the characters leaping from the page. The locations feel as if you're actually there (the author's a Windy City native who grew up close to where the book's action takes place). The dialogue sparks along, the bedroom scenes are 'real,' and the plot plays out so vividly, one can practically smell the perfume and cordite. I know gushing reviewers all say this, but I honestly couldn't put this book down. A solid five stars from this reader."

—Lori Titus, author of *Hunting in Closed Spaces* (Marradith Ryder Series) and *Black Magic Women: Terrifying Tales by Scary Sisters*

"Willie Mae Jackson's *Make it Right* is part page-turning procedural mystery, part propulsive character-driven suspense. But once the bullets begin to fly at the mass shooting that kicks off the action, you'll find yourself locked into one of the year's hottest immersive thrillers, filled with intrigue and twists. The writing style and lead character, Donovan Montgomery, conjures to mind Luke Jennings's *Codename Villanelle: Killing Eve*, now the BBC-America and Hulu hit series. But Jackson has invented a new icon for an America at a crossroads. Donovan is all about 'reckoning,' setting the record straight, making things right. I was riveted as Donovan morphs from establishment profiler to renegade, remorseless vigilante. I was on edge as Donovan brilliantly unravels the clues leading to the murderers who are so intent on turning Chicago into a wasteland of dissension and carnage. For thriller fans on the lookout for something different, *Make it Right* hits all the right buttons. Grab it!"

—Naysha Isom, MD, Family Medicine Physician

"Willie Mae Jackson's *Make It Right* is a timely, knife-edged thriller, superbly written with credible, three-dimensional characters that a reader actually cares about. The protagonist is a woman of color, an African American forensic psychiatrist and criminal profiler who is doing her best to work within the bureaucratic maze of Chicago's labyrinthine, crumbling justice system. But Montgomery Donovan (love the name!) is also evocative of Oyinkan Braithwaite's twisted sisters (as featured in *My Sister, The Serial Killer*) in so far as she is a true, functioning sociopath in every sense of the word: incredibly smart, professional to a fault, affable, a demon between the sheets, and more than capable of snapping necks and taking care of business wherever she feels justice is not doing its job well—or fast—enough. Whether Donovan is a product of nature or nurture is just a piece of the puzzle that is her makeup. The fact is that Donovan's an All-American heroine, a product of our current era who arrives just in time to help us all feel better at the end of the day. While author Jackson eschews simplistic answers and chooses some unsettling courses of action, she never loses focus on the prize: We must confront evil in all its incarnations no matter the cost or it will surely devour us alive. *Make it Right* is fast-paced, vicious (at times), intricate, and never lets up from the first page through to the very last. Grab or download your copy now!"

—Samuel L. Williams III, MD, MBA, Medical Director
Magellan Health

"Dr. Jackson's life has perfectly prepared her to write precisely this book. This is a bold, new author whose unique voice was hard-earned. Its piercing clarity will not soon be forgotten by readers."

—Maxwell Rovner, MD, JD, Forensic Psychiatrist

"If you are reading this book review, then you have already started your own hopeless, insatiable, uncontrollable literary opium that will leave you in withdrawal for the next line, chapter, and the next book/screenplay. There are many psychological and scientific protagonists such as Alex Cross, Alex Delaware, and Kay Scarpetta, but none like Dr. Donovan Montgomery. Forget that she is black. Forget that she is a Mensa genius. Forget that she is beautiful. Forget that she is a forensic psychiatrist. Forget that she is Krav Maga trained. Those are just some of the protagonist's elements that Dr. Willie Mae Jackson blends to create Dr. Donovan Montgomery. What you will not be able to forget is the unmistakable clarity, imagery, and simplistic staccato that has been absent since Ernest Hemingway. Whether be it with burnished brevity-like phrases such as, 'Everyone was impatient. Everyone was annoyed,' or emotional, intrepid, interpersonal communications such as, 'I will drag you out from under whatever dung heap you call home and show you some tough love,' Dr. Jackson accomplishes only what a contemporary Ernest Hemingway could achieve. The author uses her word artistry to expertly paint the characters of Dr. Donovan Montgomery, Maurice Brown, and the nefarious Mason Ghetz but with just enough literary ambiguity to allow the reader to project their own final description. The heroine's own duality is captured conflictually in her yin-yang struggle of good versus bad, right versus wrong, legal versus illegal as she faces an imperfect, corrupt, and morally bankrupt legal system. The reader is so captivated by Dr. Donovan's different spheres of mesmerism—intellectual, physical, emotional, and sexual—that every woman wants to be her, and every man wants to be with her. The research and factual detail of the environment will compel you to not only believe but feel you are virtually at Chicago's Daley Plaza or Lincoln Square. The story line that unfolds is clear, simple, but vigorous and powerful. There is no Faulkner-like obscurity or obfuscation. This book will complete for you W. H. Auden's declaration of stopping all the clocks and turning off the phone. You will become transported to a time zone not just of Chicago but to the world of Dr. Donovan Montgomery. My critique of this book is that I don't have another sequel immediately in my hands to prevent the literary withdrawal I experienced at the end, but then again with characters like Donovan Montgomery, I truly expect a Tolkien return."

—Andrew T. Cooley, MD - Forensic Psychiatrist; Medical Director of Eastern State Hospital; Associate Professor of Psychiatry at the University of Kentucky College of Medicine

Make It Right
Copyright © 2021 Willie Mae Jackson, MD, MA

Book design by:
Arbor Services, Inc.
www.arborservices.co/

Photography by Bauwerks
@bauwerks
@jovanka.novakovic.photographer

Printed in the United States of America

Make It Right
Willie Mae Jackson, MD, MA

1. Title 2. Author 3. Thriller

ISBN: 13: 978-1-7354262-0-4
LCCN: 2020917877

MAKE IT RIGHT

WILLIE MAE JACKSON, MD, MA

This book is dedicated to my beloved Charles Rice, III.
You are my inspiration and meaning of it all.
In memory of my beautiful mother,
thank you for being the best teacher ever.
Continue to dream, dreamers. The world is yours.

Contents

Prologue

The blood splattered across the desk was not yet dry. A slowly congealing blanket of red covered the at-a-glance blotter, golf bag–shaped pen holder, and page-a-day calendar.

A pleasant but unimpressive office, it consisted of the desk and padded chair, two chairs across from the desk, three metal file cabinets, and a small well-worn couch accompanied by a coffee table and end tables to either side.

Near the bloodied blotter stood a framed photograph of identical twin girls—both in graduation gowns and caps, both holding diplomas. This had been a candid shot evidenced by the young women's expressions as they shared an uninhibited laugh, each with an arm casually resting on the other's shoulder. Next to that frame stood another housing a photograph of a middle-aged couple posing and smiling for the camera, a photo that could have been taken by any number of department store photographers.

The body of the man in the photograph had been dragged to the corner of the room. Red track marks extended from where he had been shot to where he had been deposited. Next to him lay the corpse of a uniformed cleaning woman. The generous amount of blood produced from the holes in her chest and his head created a squishy pool beneath them on the cheap commercial carpeting.

Cradled in the comfort of the padded desk chair sat another man eating a fried egg sandwich while idly glancing at the two dead bodies. He had rolled the chair away from the desk to avoid the mess. Finishing the sandwich, he crumpled the wax paper it had been wrapped in and opened one of two duffel bags on the floor next to him: one black, one navy blue. He threw the paper in the open bag and removed a thermos. Pouring himself a cup of coffee, he enjoyed the steam for a moment before taking a cautious sip.

After brief reconsideration, he remained ultimately satisfied with having shot the man in the back of the head instead of the chest. Shooting him in the chest would have unnecessarily placed the window directly behind the desk in jeopardy, and he wanted the window intact. Shattering the glass with a bullet intended for the simple task of shooting a man at a desk would have been careless and costly.

The man swiveled the chair toward the window, lifted a pair of tactical binoculars from the black bag, and stood. With the plastic thermos cup in one hand and binoculars in the other, he gazed down on the still sleeping city. Then he placed the cup and binoculars on the chair and retrieved a bottle of Adderall from an inside jacket pocket. He popped two pills into his mouth and returned the bottle to his pocket. The coffee was no longer hot but served to wash down the drug.

Next, he pulled a circular glass cutter from the bag, the sophisticated kind designed to score the glass, cut it with surgical precision, then suction out the cut piece safely into your hand. He took his time cutting the hole in the window.

Once the hole was cut, he unzipped the navy-blue duffel bag and extracted a clamping tripod, turning his attention to setting it up. He removed one AR-15 assault rifle and then another. Walking one of the rifles over to the coffee table, he mounted the other on the tripod and aimed it out the hole in the window.

The Glock and silencer he had used to kill the businessman and cleaning woman were resting atop the foodstuffs remaining in the black duffel bag.

He checked his watch. It was five a.m. Picking up the Glock and another sandwich, he retired to the couch to put up his feet. Between bites, he took some photos of the dead bodies in the corner with his phone for his own amusement. There was nothing left to do—but wait.

Chapter One

"Three human heads in the basement freezer. Damn," said Maurice Brown. Looking restrained in a badly fitted business suit, he crossed his large, doughy arms tightly over his ample belly. "Damn," he repeated more fervently.

On an unseasonably warm October morning in downtown Chicago, he, along with Jordan Payne and Donovan Montgomery, stood sipping coffee in Daley Plaza across the street from the George W. Dunne Cook County Office Building where the two men worked—Maurice Brown as an officer of the Investigations Bureau, and Jordan Payne, an assistant to the state district attorney's office. Doctor Montgomery kept her office in Lincoln Square, but as a forensic psychiatrist, her work with various law enforcement agencies meant spending a good deal of time in the Loop.

Her most recent book about criminal profiling entitled *In Full Sight* had launched only days before, and both men were brimming with praise. Her exploration into the psychopathology and colorful, thought-provoking case studies of killers whose capture she was directly responsible for had the book topping every best-seller list.

"And it took a forensic psychiatrist to lead all those cops and detectives to that freezer in that basement. Well done, Doctor," added Maurice Brown as an addendum to his earlier comment. He extended his recyclable coffee cup to clink with hers.

"Nah, it just took Donovan," said Jordan Payne, winking at Donovan and extending his cup as well.

"All in a day's work, gentlemen," Donovan said as she clinked cardboard with one then the other.

As the two men took turns complimenting her, she noticed the cadence of Jordan Payne's speech was different than it usually was—more passionate, more animated. And though he was always polished and well-manicured, he stroked his tie and ran his hand over his low fade and Vandyke a half dozen times while chatting, a nervous tick she had observed in him on other occasions. She didn't know Maurice Brown, but she did know Jordan, and he was anxious about something. She was not. She knew what she had been hired to do.

The state's attorney's office needed to get a neo-Nazi named Mason Ghetz convicted on three counts of murder and aggravated assault. As a professional witness in twenty-five high-profile cases, Donovan's testimonies had brought in twenty-five convictions. Banking on her winning streak, they had once again solicited the doctor's services.

But another storm was brewing that inadvertently upped the ante on the outcome of the Mason Ghetz trial. A major congressional election was set to take place in three weeks, an election that included a neo-Nazi candidate on the ballot. The two events—the trial and election—had become interwoven in the minds of every Chicagoan. And, in fact, those two events scheduled to take place in tandem had captured the attention of the state and country as well.

Donovan was not clear on how her testimony or, for that matter, her professional expertise could affect the election, but she was prepared for the trial. And though she never relished small talk, she was equally prepared to let the conversation play out and allow the men to talk about her book until they were comfortable addressing why they were really there.

"You were fascinating on WGN yesterday. Seriously. Those two anchors were eating out of your hand," Jordan said, referring to a television interview she had given on a morning news show the day before. "Thought I was listening to Gavin de Becker for a minute. Then I realized Gavin de Becker isn't a beautiful black woman, so it must be Donovan Montgomery."

Donovan would have pointed out everything that was politically incorrect about that comment to nearly anyone else, but graciously accepted it from this man. Maurice grinned sheepishly and shook his head in an "Oh, brother" kind of way.

The doctor smiled. "Thanks, Counselor. I appreciate that. Gavin is not only brilliant; he's a really nice guy," she responded.

Maurice and Jordan glanced at each other, chuckling. "Of course you know Gavin de Becker," Jordan said.

"Well, of course I do," she replied with a smile.

As the three took their last sips of coffee, Jordan stared across the mottled grey concrete slabs that covered the courtyard to the expansive plaza fountain, watching the waterworks, buying a few more seconds to drum up his best sales pitch. Then in the most nonchalant manner he could muster, said, "In fact, I'd say those movie star looks of yours are shamefully wasted on the criminally insane if you weren't so damn good at what you do. But you are. You are that good."

His gaze shot to Maurice before locking intently on Donovan.

Donovan could see a subtle shift in Jordan's eyebrows that informed her he was about to turn the conversation away from books and blather and aim it directly toward the actual matter at hand, whatever that was.

Maurice had finished his coffee and was searching for a trash can. Having finished her own, Donovan took his cup, then held out her hand to Jordan. He relinquished his without comment.

She nimbly popped off the lids, placing one on top of the other, and then stacked the three cardboard cups, placing the condensed lids on top in a nearby trash receptacle. The two men glanced at each other in reference to the seamless, curious way in which she disposed of the cups, more like a close-up magic trick than someone throwing out trash. "Thanks," Maurice finally offered.

The Chicago Picasso glimmered in the bright midmorning sun. As the three ambled toward the fifty-foot sculpture, Maurice jumped in, breaking the momentary silence. "Mason Ghetz killed three people and wounded a fourth. Doesn't matter that it happened in the context of a botched drug deal. We can't have white nationalists walking on murder charges any more than we can have a neo-Nazi in Congress. There's just a whole lot riding on this conviction, Doctor."

"I've read the notes and done my homework," said Donovan as the wind whipped her long hair around the grey wool cap atop her head. "I'm doing my assessment of him today, but from what I know going into this, it shouldn't be difficult to convince a jury that Ghetz isn't psychotic; he's a killer, and perfectly capable of standing trial."

Jordan placed a hand on the shoulder of her tweed blazer, guiding her to one of the benches near the Picasso. Maurice followed suit, and over the growing din of the foot traffic beginning to fill the plaza, said, "There's a good chance Ghetz is going to have another murder on his tab. The fourth guy is in a coma. If he lives, he'll probably be a vegetable. He's twenty-four. We all know that's what the trial is about—on paper. But given Mason

Ghetz is a neo-Nazi and an active member of the Aryan Brotherhood and all of his victims were black … You do see where I'm going with this."

She nodded. "You don't need me to convince a jury that he's a racist. His past and current alliances are well documented. But his motivation and mental clarity, the fact that the murders and attempted murder were premeditated and not self-defense, which is what he is alleging, I believe I can explain that to them in a way that all twelve people will be confident that they're making the right decision to put him away."

Jordan guffawed. "Well, as one African American to another, I'm just saying it's getting a little harder than usual to be black in Chicago right now. Let's sit here. I want to keep an eye out for Jen." He was referring to Jen Park, the Cook County state's attorney and the woman they were waiting to meet.

Jordan sat down and added, "This was the first-degree murder of black men because they were black men, okay? This was a hate crime. He wasn't in any danger. Maybe they were trying to steal OxyContin from Ghetz, maybe they were buying the Oxy from him, but either way, there was no threat. They were running for their lives when he fatally shot all three of them in the back of their heads. Now, as far as I know, when you chase somebody down and shoot 'em in the back of the head, that's first-degree murder."

Maurice turned sideways a few inches on the bench so as to speak to Donovan eye to eye. "We don't need for you to explain to the jury why he did what he did in that parking lot. We need for you to make sure they understand who he is."

"I hear that," Donovan said. "Of course, *why* he did it may be the best way to show them *exactly* who he is."

Maurice pursed his lips, contemplating their expert witness's rather cryptic assertion. He wasn't sure what she meant, but asking her to explain didn't seem necessary. She clearly had a handle on Mason Ghetz and how she would be presenting her findings.

Donovan, on the other hand, needed a little more clarification on the coffee klatch she had been summoned to that morning.

"So, I understand why you two would want to check in with me face-to-face before the trial, and the coffee was very good, thank you, Jordan, but why am I meeting with the state's attorney, again?"

Jordan checked his watch and glanced out into traffic at the mention of his boss's imminent arrival. "You mean the first African American woman to ever grace the Cook County state's attorney's office? Jen has done a whole lot right for this state. She might have made a couple of notable missteps, but you know the one thing everybody can agree on about Jen Park? She's not a neo-Nazi. Now, some people may see this election as a black and white issue, but we don't see it that way. This isn't about black and white. This is about right and wrong."

Maurice chimed in. "Look, Doctor, this election in three weeks is absolutely crucial in the fight against white supremacy taking a foothold in politics, not only here in Illinois but in the country. We have to get Jen reelected, period."

She nodded. "I'm still waiting for the part where you explain how I fit into this."

Jordan crossed his long legs and unbuttoned his suit jacket. "Donovan, in that last election, twenty-five percent of Illinois voters in the Third Congressional District voted for Sinclair White. You remember Sinclair White? A proud member of the American Nazi Party and Holocaust denier? Twenty-five percent. This time it's the GOP, but in the past, it's been the Democrats. Even those 'strange Lyndon LaRouche acolytes,' as the *Trib* called them, pledged their goddamn allegiance. Morality and ethics aside, these mongrels are a danger. It's up to us to stop them—one devil at a time."

Maurice Brown, legs apart, elbows on knees, and large hands clasped between them, dropped his head in a hangdog way, then lifted it and softly said, "Every law enforcement agency will tell you that white nationalism is firmly on the rise. There is a very real movement afoot to regroup and rebrand after that rally in Charlottesville. That was not an anomaly, Doctor. It was a calling card. They're waiting. They're organizing. Believe it."

Donovan and Maurice sat shoulder to shoulder and eye to eye. "What do you want me to do?" she asked.

Jordan responded to her question, this time with no decorum and both gloves off. "We need to send a clear message to those motherfuckers that they're not welcome here. Ghetz is the messenger. Just get us a conviction."

Directing his attention to the street, he stood up as an SUV pulled over to the curb. "Here we go. That's Jen."

Maurice and Donovan scrambled to their feet and turned toward the street as well. They watched as the driver got out and opened the door for Jen Park and requisite bodyguard.

A tall woman made more imposing in heels, she and her bodyguard stood at the curb taking in the crowd milling around the plaza. Jordan waved. Spotting her two staff members and Donovan, she smiled broadly and began to walk in their direction, her bodyguard making it somewhat easier to maneuver through the crowd.

Maurice, Jordan, and Donovan moved to greet Jen Park as she approached them. When they were all in easy proximity to one another, she said, "Morning, gentlemen." Then extending her hand to Donovan, said, "Doctor Montgomery, it's so nice to meet you."

Donovan shook Jen's hand firmly. "State's Attorney, the pleasure is mine."

Gunfire stopped the conversation. Bullets swarmed into Daley Plaza like wasps. And like wasps, they descended without warning and refused to be outrun.

Maurice Brown watched in slow motion as the bodyguard next to Jen Park drew his gun and threw his arm across the state's attorney's chest before falling dead at her feet. He saw her stare at her employee and friend, frozen in disbelief. Maurice Brown himself remained standing a good five seconds after being riddled with bullets before he hit the ground.

In those first moments, as each unthinkable, surreal horror rolled out in freeze-frame before the crowd had yet processed that they were being slaughtered *en masse*, Donovan had already shoved Jordan under one of the benches, pushed Jen Park to the concrete, and instinctively thrown herself over the woman.

The lucky ones ran and screamed while the less lucky were randomly executed. The families and city workers, shopkeepers and city hall staffers dropped in their tracks as the plaza grew cluttered with bodies and blood.

Chapter Two

By nine a.m., every cop in Chicago seemed to be in Daley Plaza. The wide variety of food trucks that are an integral part of the plaza's charm were wedged between dozens of paramedics, ambulances, and squad cars positioned among the dead and wounded.

Television and radio crews, as well as print publications, vied for position, each attempting to be as near the carnage as possible. TV cameras and photographers made an effort to capture the devastation by zooming in on the tears and panic washing over every face in the crowd.

As someone well known by the media, and a media darling at the time, Donovan was sought out by more than one journalist at the scene. Some wanted nothing more than a quote from her, anything they could use as a sound bite to easily upload and replay throughout the news cycle. Others wanted more.

A reporter from the *Chicago Tribune* had the doctor engaged in recounting the events that had just unfolded, spitting a long list of questions at her in rapid succession. Donovan remained collected and discerning in sharing her opinions about shooter versus shooters, the logical vantage point (or points) of the attack, and possible motivation. She was no one's fool and could not be bullied by the press for statements, no matter how respectful and professional the interrogation.

"I would prefer not to speculate at this time" and "I'm sure the authorities are looking into that" were among the phrases she rotated throughout the impromptu "interview." As she talked to the reporter, she kept an eye on a responsive Jen Park beneath a shroud of cameras being treated by an EMT over by the fountain while the bodies of Jen's bodyguard and Maurice Brown were strapped to gurneys and loaded into a coroner's van.

The reporter turned off the recorder and glanced over his shoulder in the direction Donovan was looking. "A bullet grazed her right ear. Close call, but she's okay," he said.

"I'm so glad," Donovan responded.

"I was over there before I cornered you. No offense," he said. "She's sticking with 'No comment' and 'I'm fine' for the moment."

"Smart woman," the doctor said.

He nodded, taking in the morbid exhibition around him. Raising his voice to compete with the din of the frantic crowd, he added, "You know, Doctor, I think I'm losing that detached professionalism I've always been so proud of."

Donovan could see two other reporters with cameramen in tow making their way toward her. Touching the arm of his jacket, she said, "Good for you," and started walking.

She was aiming for the Block 37 parking lot on State Street where she'd left her Prius that morning. She didn't get there. In fact, she didn't get more than a few feet away before the news crews stopped her in her tracks. Jordan Payne caught up with her as well.

As he approached, he removed a hanky from his pocket and wiped what he thought was sweat from his brow. The white linen in his hand turned red. He had apparently cut himself on the concrete bench. Blood trickled down his cheek and stained his white shirt collar. His other hand was also bleeding and had sullied his suit jacket.

Attempting to appear composed for the media, he took Donovan's elbow and made their apologies, promising that they would both release statements as soon as possible, and gracefully pulled her away from the press.

Keeping a firm grip on her arm, he led her briskly toward the glass doors that would get them to his office in the Daley Center Building and out of the fray. "It's only because of you that Jen and I are alive," Jordan said. "You know that, right? You saved our asses out there. You're like some kind of gravity-defying ninja baby or some shit. I never get used to it."

Without stopping, she said, "I'm not going to go out with you, Jordan."

Still dabbing at his wounds, he tried to smile. "Yeah, well, we'll see about that, but definitely not today. I want to look somewhat better than this when I get around to that. Less blood on the Armani."

When they neared the building, he stopped and turned her toward him. "Girl, are you okay?"

Donovan peered into the eyes of this man still shaken from the bloodbath they had both witnessed. His reaction was—*normal*. But Donovan was more intrigued than shaken. She knew that she was wired differently than most people. She also knew that were she not, she couldn't do the kind of work she did, and certainly not with such stellar results. Giving Jordan a genuine, believable nod and smile, she said, "I am, Counselor. Really."

He nodded back, studying her face and arriving at the conclusion that she truly was all right. Straightening his tie and stroking his Vandyke, he said, "Okay, I think I'm breathing normally now. What the fuck happened out there, Donovan?"

She observed the mob of survivors and considered the victims she had seen: all colors and ages, well-dressed city officials and T-shirt tourists alike. There was no obvious connection. The dead and wounded represented every walk of life. What was the throughline?

"Well, it could have been a hate crime, Jordan. There is an ever-expanding number of hate groups who have made their presence known in Illinois over the past four years: anti-Muslim, anti-LGBT, and as you well know, an ever-growing number of neo-Nazis. There are even general hate organizations."

He knew of the groups and knew that one of them being behind the shooting was a strong possibility. Though they didn't have a body count yet, the sheer size of the slaughter would suggest something like that. But Donovan had more options for consideration.

"On the other hand, it could've been some lone wolf who just bought a new automatic he wanted to play with. And, Jordan"—she took an extra beat before offering a third possibility—"this might have been an assassination attempt, and the state's attorney might well have been the target."

Jordan studied the cut on his hand while rolling those scenarios over in his head.

"Or maybe it's just Chicago's turn." A voice interjected itself into their conversation before the man attached to the voice joined them.

Detective James DuMont now stood beside the two who were still standing directly outside of Daley Center. A short man with thinning hair and piercing blue eyes, he readjusted his well-worn stingy brim fedora and deposited the notepad and pen he was holding in the inside pocket of his trench coat.

"Detective," Donovan said with a nod.

"Doctor," he responded flatly.

Donovan and Detective DuMont had a history, and the residue from it clung to both. Though she predominantly worked for law enforcement, Donovan had, on rare occasions, helped "clean up" some of the less-than-savory chapters in the department's past. It was her testimony that had put away a fledgling detective who happened to be DuMont's partner at the time. He never forgave her. He remained convinced that he could have saved the young cop and turned his life around without dragging out his dirty laundry, which ruined any chance of having a future with the force.

Donovan knew him to be a top-notch investigator. She never understood how he could, in good conscience, persist in justifying his former partner's behavior, behavior that was clearly unjustifiable, how he could continue to bend cold reality into a warmer version that he was more comfortable with. But only when it came to that case had she observed such a hiccup in the detective's work ethic. Beyond this one glaring glitch, James DuMont was great at what he did.

And though his distaste and distrust of Donovan Montgomery never flagged, he recognized her work to be necessary and privately applauded her penchant for solving crimes not by the book, but by her own book. That was something they had in common. He respected her.

"Columbine, Sandy Hook, Orlando, Vegas. I can't remember all of them. Chicago was bound to draw the short straw sooner or later," DuMont said, his gaze volleying between Donovan and Jordan.

"Detective DuMont, this is Jordan Payne, an assistant state's attorney. Counselor, this is Detective James DuMont, lead investigator for the Cook County Crimes Unit." The men shook hands.

The detective inspected his palm after shaking Jordan's hand. Jordan drew back his hand, which was still seeping from the rather deep wound he had received earlier. DuMont grabbed a hanky from his pants pocket and wiped the blood from his palm. "What a mess out there. Better get that looked at. Grab one of the EMTs. They'll clean it and dress it for you."

"Jesus, I'm sorry, Detective." Jordan retrieved his own hanky and wrapped it around his hand. "I don't know what I fell on. Maybe a nail or glass or something. My apologies."

"No apology necessary. I've seen a lot worse than that today." He rubbed the back of his neck and shook his head.

"Do they have a body count?" Donovan asked.

"Not yet," the detective answered. "Must be a couple dozen at least. I understand we lost Maurice Brown. That's a shame. Good man, Maurice. Fifteen years on the job. Good cop." He looked directly at Donovan and added, "Real good cop. No two ways about it."

Jordan's eyes appeared glassy when the detective mentioned Maurice. "We were standing with him. We had just had coffee with him. Big man like that just dropping in a dead heap. I didn't realize he'd been on the job that long."

Thinking about Maurice brought the gravity of the morning's events front and center in Payne's mind. Yes, there were questions that needed to be answered. Yes, there was still a trial and election that needed to be addressed. But he had nearly died only an hour before. And he had watched so many people die around him, including Maurice Brown. "Not like it is in the movies, is it?" He turned to Donovan.

"What's not, Counselor?" she asked.

"Death," he responded.

The detective cleared his throat and scratched his head, scanning the periphery of the plaza then up at the surrounding structures. Donovan was doing the same.

"I think the shots came from the Chicago Temple Building there at the northwest corner. It would have provided the best vantage point," she offered.

Detective DuMont's attention shifted from the skyline to Donovan Montgomery. "Well, we'll sort all that out, Doctor." Then he extended his hand again to Jordan. "Good to meet you." Jordan extended his unbloodied hand. "You get that looked at. Any one of these folks would be happy to take care of it." Touching the brim of his hat to Donovan as he walked away, he muttered, "Doctor," and made his way back into the crowd.

Once again on their own, Donovan and Jordan watched DuMont leave. "That nice detective can't stand you," he said to Donovan. "What did you do to him?"

Now facing one another, she straightened the twisted lapel on his jacket. "Maybe I'll tell you all about it someday."

Considering what the detective had said, Jordan glanced down again at his hand. "Donovan, I'd be a fool not to get one of these professionals to look at this. Maybe I can find somebody who's not dealing with—bigger issues right now, and see if maybe I need a stitch or something. Right?" He looked to her for approval on this decision.

"Yes, Counselor. That is exactly what you should do."

He started off, then turned around. "You still meeting with Ghetz today?"

"As far as I know. Jury selection is happening as we speak. I don't think they're going to postpone the trial for this, but they might. Hopefully, they'll stay on schedule. I'm ready to meet him, Jordan. I'll keep you posted."

He approached her, this time close enough to whisper in her ear. "Do that. You hear me? Be careful." He allowed his mouth to hover close to her cheek for a moment, then took off into the crowd.

As she watched Jordan disappear, she caught a glimpse of another man, a man who had been her champion from her first day on the job eight years prior. Alfredo Ramos, older, slightly weathered, and one of the few people Donovan deemed to be as astute as herself, was the Cook County medical examiner.

She had assessed her first dead body in his examining room with him at her side and had watched him perform myriad autopsies as she shared her findings on various aspects of each murder or accident. In addition to his tenure and acumen on the job, he was also one of the few people she considered to be a friend, a word that to her meant trust, therefore it was a word she seldom used.

Currently, he was wheeling a gurney to an ambulance, the face of the person on the gurney covered by a sheet. He saw her at about the same moment she saw him. She waved. He smiled.

Eager to get out of there and back to her car, she thought about just calling him later, but he was right there, and she did want to hear his thoughts on the deadly event. "Hold up, luv. I'll be over in a moment," he yelled from across the concrete tile.

When he finished getting the gurney in the ambulance, he sauntered over in her direction. She thought how composed he appeared among the despair and confusion.

He kissed her on the cheek while simultaneously removing rubber gloves.

"Sorry to see you, darling. Were you here when it happened?"

"I was. Never seen anything like it."

"Isn't it frightening that there are still fresh vistas of horror unexplored? And, by the way, I have never seen anything like it myself, and I've been doing this for a very long time. You're truly all right?"

"I am," she said, then methodically continued. "I watched a man die that I was talking to moments before. I was standing next to him. Jordan was there. The three of us: me, Jordan, and Maurice Brown were about to meet with the state's attorney. Just as she approached, the sky lit up. Ms. Park's bodyguard didn't get his gun drawn before dying at her feet."

Alfredo knew she was not recounting the events because they had overwhelmed her; she was walking herself through it again, slowly, hunting for the killer's or killers' opportunity, vantage point, and motive.

"Alfredo, this could have been any number of things, but"—she indicated the Picasso, which she was well behind at present but which had been directly in front and to the side of her when the shooting took place—"was the Picasso hit?"

The medical examiner wasn't sure and seemed intrigued by the question. "No one has mentioned it. One of the officers might know. What's on your mind?"

She shrugged. "It's just—a very large work of art. Sticks up in the sky fifty feet. If someone or a handful of someones wanted to randomly gun down a large group of people, it seems there was a pretty specific area being targeted."

Alfredo Ramos peered pensively around the plaza. "Pretty sloppy marksmanship if this was performed as a targeted shooting, don't you think?"

"Indeed." She adjusted her tweed jacket to keep out the cold wind that had dropped a good twenty degrees over the last hour and a half. "Or brilliantly diverting."

Donovan and Alfredo talked awhile longer about what the next steps would be with all the bodies being deposited in his office, as well as all the families attached to those bodies. "Breaks my heart," he said warmly.

"You have your work cut out for you, my friend," Donovan mused. In the courtyard, many of the media crews had left or were packing up. The wounded remaining were being consoled and treated. The screams had tempered to moans and tears.

Snapping on fresh gloves, Alfredo said, "This is the office today, I'm afraid. Mark practically detained me from leaving the house. I keep telling him that by the time I'm needed, the danger is long gone."

She tried to smile and touched the shoulder of his lab coat. "Be glad you have somebody looking out for you, Alfie."

He regarded her sweetly, gave her a peck on the cheek, and started to follow an EMT to a nearby body. He stopped and turned around. "You still meeting with Mason Ghetz today?" he asked.

Donovan nodded. "I don't think they'll postpone the trial because of this, but they might. Unless I hear otherwise, yes, I'm meeting with him at one o'clock."

Alfredo retracted his steps and stood again in front of her. "You want a police escort to the jail?"

"No," she answered without consideration. But then she thought through his offer. Though she was not afraid for her safety, an escort would mean fielding traffic and getting processed into the jail much faster—and she had much to do before meeting Mason Ghetz. "You know, Alfie, that would be great."

"Good. That way we'll both feel a little safer." He motioned for a cop to come over who Donovan happened to know, and an escort was procured. "Thank you, Benjamin. Just get her to her car and follow her home. Then make sure she gets from her home to 26th and Cal."

The cop understood and escorted Donovan to her car.

"Bit much, don't you think?" she shouted back to Alfredo who was stepping toward the body he had left moments before.

"Just enough," he said.

Chapter Three

Donovan made good time getting to the Cook County Courthouse Criminal Division for her appointment with Mason Ghetz. The cop assigned to escort her kept his lights flashing, and that was enough for every other vehicle on the road to make way for the small procession that consisted of his motorcycle and her Prius.

The doctor fought to focus on Ghetz and his trial as she drove from the Loop to Chicago's Westside where the killer waited, but the mass shooting she had witnessed and barely escaped only hours earlier still monopolized her thoughts. Why and how the slaughter took place were among the questions she could not seem to file away for a later, more convenient time.

Her focus became more clear the closer she got to her appointment. The foreboding landscape always demanded her full attention. Here, the streets held no charm. There were no shops or eateries, just a bleak canvas of grey nothingness surrounding one of Chicago's most infamous destinations, 26th and Cal.

That's what the locals and law enforcement called the Cook County Courthouse Criminal Division located at 26th Street and California Avenue, which consisted of two imposing buildings adjacent to the Cook County Jail. The infamy of the place: the celebrated trials and gangland history had inspired novelists and filmmakers alike. It had also led to a steady parade of guided tours through its halls, courtrooms, and dark history.

But, other than those people wanting the vicarious experience of walking through a world they would otherwise never see, nobody visited 26th and Cal unless they had to.

The seven-story limestone edifice that housed the criminal courthouse had been open for business since April Fool's Day, 1929. The much newer twelve-story tower next door was the Criminal Court Administration Building, which housed a variety of offices from public defender to social services. One of those offices was the Cook County Forensic Clinical Services Department. That's where Donovan was headed.

The assessment of Mason Ghetz was scheduled for one o'clock. She also planned to check in on Vivian White, a patient of hers who was being held on attempted murder. It was twelve thirty when she and her escort pulled into the parking lot. Donovan thanked the officer, sent him on his way, and walked toward the concrete steps that would lead her to the glass doors of the Criminal Court Administration Building.

The austere, Greek and Roman–inspired architecture of the Criminal Court Building to the right stood in sharp contrast to the modernism of the other, with "Cook County Criminal Court" carved atop its weathered stone pillars. Donovan always took a moment, whenever she was called there, to admire this antiquated beauty that consistently hosted between ten and twelve murder trials daily, more than any other courthouse in the United States. On this occasion, she gave it only a passing glance as she ascended the stairs to the administration building, making her way through a crowd of people milling around outside.

The scene in the lobby was always chaotic with throngs of people waiting for their opportunity to speak to someone. Twenty-plus departments and agencies operated therein. Everyone was impatient. Everyone was annoyed.

The energy that filled the lobby was palpable. Though Donovan had grown immune to it, she was still aware of it each time she entered.

Before proceeding to anywhere in the building, visitors, as well as those employed by the various agencies, were required to remove external belongings and pass through a metal detector. Those who supervised these screenings were not hired because of their customer service skills nor their warmth. Aloof at best and venomous on occasion, these supervisors commonly added to the frustration of the souls being processed through. Of course, on occasion one of them would seize some weapon that did not belong in the building. And because of this, the supervisors were a "necessary evil."

There were two lines for the screenings: one for visitors and the other for employees. Donovan stood in one line, and directly across from her stood a young woman in the other. The young woman was pleading with the agent to let her pass, as she had been asked to step back and reenter the metal detector three times. She had a vague but detectable Midwestern dialect. The doctor wondered if the young woman might have been from Missouri or Ohio.

The young woman's voice rose and her movements became more erratic each time she was asked to remove something else and step back through.

In response, the agent said, "Get your fucking hands off of the motherfucking conveyor belt and walk your ass back through this goddamn machine. And if you don't keep your voice down and do exactly what I say, and I mean exactly what I say, I'm going to have your sorry ass thrown out of here. Then you ain't gonna get to your boyfriend at all. You hear me? Do you *hear—me?*"

The young woman froze. With tears brimming from her glassy eyes, she slowly and methodically felt her head for bobby pins and her pockets for some buried metal trinket she might have forgotten to remove.

Donovan exited her line as the young woman finally finished in the other. Their eyes met as each gathered their respective belongings from the conveyor belt.

"Don't let that woman upset you. This place can be upsetting enough. You okay?" Donovan asked her.

"I—I've never been in a place like this. My boyfriend ain't never done nothing crazy before. I don't know what I'm supposed to do." The tears fell freely now. "I don't even know where I'm supposed to go or where he is or anything."

As the young woman cried and explained her circumstance, Donovan placed her hand on her shoulder and led her toward a desk. "These folks here are going to tell you exactly where he is and what you're supposed to do. I promise. Okay?"

The young woman's face went from contorted, child-like horror to something calmer as Donovan spoke and gently nodded affirmatively. "Thank you," the young woman finally managed to say as Donovan signed in at the same desk before starting for the elevator. "Thank you so much. This place … This place is …" The young woman was at a loss for words.

"This place is Chicago," Donovan said with a smile.

The Forensic Clinical Services Department on the tenth floor was where the doctor conducted forensic examinations for those awaiting trial. This examination was designed to determine whether the person was competent to stand trial, understood what they were on trial for, and in Ghetz's case, to determine that it was not self-defense, as he claimed, but the cold-blooded, premeditated murder of three men and the wounding of another.

The Cook County Jail held between nine and ten thousand men and women at any given time. On this day, Mason Ghetz was among them.

With his wrists and ankles shackled, guards escorted Ghetz from his maximum-security cell through the underground tunnel system that connected the jail to the courthouses and administration building. This was the procedure for all detainees being transported within the confines of 26th and Cal.

Black guards stood at either side of the white nationalist as they entered a tunnel elevator in tandem. When the elevator door opened, Ghetz was deposited into a large holding cell on the tenth floor. Sitcoms from the eighties usually lit the screen of an old television mounted to one wall. But on that day, the mass shooting in Daley Plaza had monopolized the airwaves. Orange plastic benches filled the otherwise drab room, and at least a dozen other men sat on those benches watching footage of the gruesome event and waiting for their names to be called. Some let out small cheers. Others remained nonplussed by the news being broadcast.

At times, the detainees and inmates transferred to this room waited no more than a few minutes before being called in. Often, they waited for several hours. Never fewer than four or five correctional officers patrolled the holding cell and halls adjacent to the room. Alert and ready, they paced back and forth—watching. That day, every officer was particularly vigilant.

Ghetz positioned himself as best he could to catch a glimpse of the mounted TV screen. He sat unconcerned through clips of the dead and wounded and the tearful tirades of those who had barely survived the ordeal. But then a news bite aired of Donovan Montgomery speaking to a reporter. Ghetz jerked on the bench, craning his neck to be sure that his eyes were not deceiving him. They were not.

His name was called. Guards ushered the shackled man from the large, busy cell to a small, private one.

The space Mason Ghetz was moved to had a concrete floor and clear plastic walls, making it possible for guards to observe what went on inside its confines at all times. In the plastic room were a metal desk and two metal stools. Once the guards had positioned Ghetz on one of those stools, they handcuffed him to it and anchored a chain from his waist to a heavy steel ring on the concrete floor.

The guards then left the room and Donovan was called in. Both would remain directly outside the door once the doctor was in-conference. Donovan knew the procedure. She had performed it on multiple occasions. But the clear plastic cell never ceased to inspire a certain level of dark poetry in her. And as she approached the door, she could feel it, same as she had the time before and the time before that.

The cell was transparent by design, but the walls somehow managed to reflect all of the anger, guilt, and fear of every soul who had been asked to share its story within those confines. Some were tortured; some were apathetic. Regardless, every conversation stuck like pus to those chamber walls: all of the alibis, each confession, every plea.

As she funneled away those thoughts and approached, Donovan saw Ghetz chained in place, staring straight ahead. When the guard opened the door to the chamber and allowed her entrance, Ghetz turned toward her. She had seen many photographs of the man in preparation for the assessment and trial, but reality dwarfed what those cameras had captured.

Tattoos covered one side of his neck and part of his face atop a small, wiry frame. The coal-black color of his crepe-like hair had been store bought and badly applied with dye stains still visible at his temples and tops of his ears. Ancient pockmarks mapped both cheeks, and the fleshy bags under his tiny grey eyes were larger than the eyes themselves. These features along with the bright orange jumpsuit he had been issued by the State of Illinois conspired against him under harsh fluorescent lights.

Mason Ghetz was notably shocked to see Donovan Montgomery. She could tell by the way he recoiled and straightened his spine when he saw her. His reaction was subtle but did not escape her. Perhaps he was simply readying himself for the assessment. Perhaps he was thrown by her ethnicity or gender. Whatever the reason, the expression that slowly crawled across his chalky face was nothing short of revulsion.

"Good afternoon, Mr. Ghetz. I'm Doctor Montgomery. How are you today?" Donovan asked while taking a seat on the metal stool across from the man. She removed a notepad and pen from her purse and crossed her legs beneath the metal desk. Ignoring that he hadn't answered her, she continued unbothered.

"I'm a forensic psychiatrist. Do you know what that is, Mr. Ghetz? Do you know why I'm here?" the doctor asked. Ghetz said nothing.

"I'm a psychiatrist who works with law enforcement to determine things about people, such as yourself, before they stand trial. I'm here to gather information and make that information available to the court. In your case, the court asks for confirmation that you're mentally fit to stand trial, that you adequately understand the court process, and will be able to work with your attorney. May I ask a few questions?" She peered across the desk at the man who was staring back at her.

"I'm going to need a response for the record," she added, realizing he was content to give her none. He cracked his neck on one side and then the other. Breaking the silence while maintaining eye contact with Donovan, he barked once like a mad dog. The doctor's muscles contracted involuntarily. Ghetz laughed. She glanced over at the guards. They both shifted their weight from one foot to the other, studying her intently, ready to end the session should she give a sign. She did not.

Donovan grinned and raised an eyebrow. She knew that if she called him out on his behavior, she was unlikely to get any informative conversation from him. So, she opted to file her impulse to ask if his rabies vaccine was current and proceeded with the examination.

"Though I am a psychiatrist, I'm not here in any doctor/patient capacity. I'm not going to be counseling you or treating you. And I promise I'm not going to be prescribing any meds. I'm hoping you will answer some questions for me about your past and present that will cast some light on the events that happened on the night of October 2nd, the night you encountered those men in the parking lot."

He leaned over as far as the chains would allow and spit on the concrete.

"I'd like to talk with you about some details I've come across that relate to your childhood, ones that might have colored your view of the circumstances that night."

Ghetz parted his lips enough to hiss at the doctor. He hissed like a snake until he ran out of air. One long *sssssss*. Hissing and barking were moves Donovan had not seen before in her former assessments. But something about this man made her think that was not the first time he had expressed himself that way.

"And I'd like to learn more about your mom's schizophrenia, your dad's anger issues, your struggles with depression, any traumas that might have influenced—"

"Fuck you."

"... addictions and withdrawals ..."

"Fuck you."

"... other medical conditions ..."

"Fuck you."

"Mr. Ghetz, I haven't asked you anything yet. I'm letting you know what the assessment will be about if you choose to proceed." Donovan took a moment to shake off the rapid-fire insults Ghetz shot off before starting in again. "I want to hear from you where your head was on the night you shot those men."

"Fuck you, I already told the fucking cops."

The doctor slapped both palms on the table, making a large bang with a small gesture. "There are no cops here, Mr. Ghetz. This is just you and me talking. Just you and me. And you are not obligated to answer any of the questions I'm about to ask you. Or you can answer some of them and choose to not answer others. It's up to you. But either way, your participation or lack of participation will be documented and submitted to the court. Do you understand, Mr. Ghetz?"

He furrowed his brow, then manipulated the handcuffs to place one finger to his chin in a mock "what should I do" kind of way.

"And you need to be clear that this conversation is not confidential. What we talk about today will be included in a written report, and my assessments, based on already recorded information and this conversation, will contribute to my testimony at your trial."

Ghetz smiled, exposing a mouthful of tobacco-stained, Chiclet gum–sized teeth except for one gold incisor up front. "You gonna speak at my trial?"

"Yes," Donovan said, readjusting herself on the stool. "Yes, I am."

He turned to look through one plastic wall at the guards standing outside the chamber, hands clasped, observing. "Damned if I do, damned if I don't." His toothy smile now stretched from ear to ear as he softly chuckled.

Donovan tapped the pen against the metal to redirect his attention. "Now that you understand the process and the kinds of things that will be discussed, do you wish to proceed, Mr. Ghetz?" she asked.

He slowly shifted his eyes from the guards back to her. The toothy, maniacal smile had disintegrated and been replaced with something much darker as he responded, "Do you?"

Chapter Four

Still chained to the floor, Mason Ghetz remained seated as the doctor signaled to the guards that she was ready to leave. That's how it always went: the doctor left first, then the detainee was ushered back to his or her cell through the underground tunnels that led back to the Cook County Jail.

Much to her surprise, Ghetz ended up participating in the assessment. Only twice more did he inject odd animal noises for her to interpret. In that he smiled broadly each time he did this, she deduced he was playing a kind of game with her. It wasn't a fun game, but a game, nevertheless. Regardless, she had what she needed to write the assessment and was eager to get back to her office to do so.

"See you real soon," he said as she exited the plastic room.

Donovan hurried to make her way back through the busy lobby of the Criminal Court Administration Building. She practically leaped back down the concrete stairs and took off in a sprint for her car. She felt the push to get away from the building as quickly as possible. She glanced down at her suit jacket and skirt, then at her stocking and shoes. No rips, no stains, not even a wayward crease. She appeared to be unsullied, but she felt dirty. This was different for Donovan. She had not experienced this particular reaction on any other occasion.

After twenty-five high-profile cases and myriad others that were made less public, Donovan had snuck and pried her way into the hidden corners of many criminal minds. From infanticide to necrophilia, occult conspiracies to ritual killings, she had been up close and personal with the rape, murder, and madness that permeated civilized society. She had met only a few who made her as uneasy as Mason Ghetz, and she couldn't place her finger on why.

She was at her car before remembering that she had told Vivian White she would be seeing her that day. With the shooting in the morning and the unsettling experience with Ghetz, Donovan Montgomery had nearly dropped the ball. But Donovan wasn't about to break a promise, most especially to someone as fragile and alone as Vivian White.

Turning on her heels, she returned to the jailhouse next to the administration building and asked to see her patient. The guard informed the doctor that Vivian had been moved two days prior. Donovan was told that Vivian apparently lashed out at another inmate and had to be separated. "Why wasn't I called?" Donovan asked the guard. An apathetic shrug of the shoulders told her everything she needed to know. "Well, we have an appointment. Please take me to wherever you have her."

The two had first met in the same jail seven months prior when Vivian was arrested for the attempted murder of a woman who lived on her street in South Deering. Her bipolar disorder, an illness that she had struggled with throughout her life, had escalated upon her incarceration. Donovan thought she could help the young woman and took her on as a patient.

Initially, Vivian didn't speak at all, and Donovan spent several sessions having one-sided conversations before she was able to engage Vivian in a dialogue. But eventually, she did. And the person that the doctor had come to know could be as warm as she was funny. Those were her good days. On her bad days, she grew sullen and despondent, sometimes angry to the point of aggression. Unfortunately, most of the time, Vivian simply withdrew, becoming almost invisible—at least to herself.

Donovan was familiar with Vivian's isolation and the reason for it.

Her younger sister Rose had died two years prior. Schoolmates discovered the body behind a toilet in the girls' bathroom at Washington High. A fatal dose of methamphetamine was the alleged cause of death. Rose had been fifteen years old when it happened; Vivian was twenty. She identified the body, as their mother had left years before and their father disappeared shortly after, leaving no forwarding address.

Rose had no history with drugs of any kind, so the death seemed like something closer to murder in Vivian's mind. But the cops were happy enough with letting the file read "self-inflicted accidental overdose," as South Deering was rife with dealers and derelicts.

Two neighbor women began taunting Vivian on a regular basis, casting lowbrow insults and vague innuendoes that hinted that her self-interests were somehow responsible for Rose's death. Tormenting her seemed to humor them. One day, Vivian had had enough and took a kitchen knife to one of the women, slashing her throat before the other woman wrestled her to the ground and held her there until the cops showed up.

Now, Donovan stood outside the cell that held Vivian White, "Vee" to her friends.

Stepping close to the small window cut into the door, the doctor peered inside, locating her patient. Crouched in a corner with her arms wrapped tightly around her waist, the young woman sat with her back against one wall and leaning with her face pressed against the other.

"Vee … Vee, it's Doctor Montgomery. How are you doing? Can you hear me? I told you I'd come see you today, remember? Nobody contacted me about them moving you or I would have been here sooner. Vee, you want to tell me about it?"

She waited, but Vivian White did not move a muscle, let alone speak.

"You have a voice, Vee. You need to use it."

The young woman's head slowly lifted away from the wall as she focused on the familiar eyes peering in through the small opening. Donovan waited for a response to follow the recognition. The woman shook her head no, her lips now pinched in a tight knot.

Encouraged that she had finally provoked a reaction, she tried again.

"Yeah, you have a voice. And I believe that if you could release some of that rage another way ... Look, I don't even know what happened. I'd really rather hear it from you, Vivian. I want to hear about it from you, okay? Can you do that for me? I can help you, Vee. Maybe get you moved out of here and into a ward or ... get you into the Cermak. Wouldn't that be better?"

The young woman leaped up from the concrete corner as if she had been shot from a cannon and lunged at the steel door separating them. The movement was so dramatic that Donovan instinctively jerked back for a moment. Then she gently stepped up to the door again, placing her hands to either side of the hole through which they could communicate. On the opposite side, Vivian did the same.

In whisper-speak, the young woman finally found her tongue. "They tellin' me I ain't got no voice. They tellin' me that I better not say one more goddamn thing or things gonna get real bad for me in here."

Donovan squinted slightly, then relaxed her face. "Who? Who told you that?"

Vivian again shook her head. "All of 'em. All of 'em wish that I would shut the fuck up. Maybe they scared. Maybe they devils. But I just shut my mouth. I shut my mouth and I ain't opened it for the past two days ever since they stuck me in this cell."

Donovan removed her hands from the door and slid them into her pockets, readjusting her stance. "Are you taking your meds?"

"No, ma'am. No meds. I think they stopped giving them to me right after I saw you a couple weeks ago."

Anger washed over Donovan at hearing the medications were being ignored, but she wasn't surprised by the neglect. "Well, we're going to fix that today, okay? Vivian, what happened the day before yesterday? Why did they think it was necessary to separate you?"

"Everybody knows."

"Knows what?"

"That he's in here."

Donovan's skin pricked and a shiver ran through her. "Everybody knows that *who* is in here?" she asked, hoping that she didn't already know the answer.

"Mason Ghetz, Doctor Montgomery. Mason Ghetz. Half of them think he's a monster, and the other half think he's a motherfuckin' rock star."

Donovan knew how the prison system worked. She knew that the channels through which news traveled on the inside were complex, expedient, and unstoppable.

"What does Mason Ghetz have to do with this, Vee? You need to tell me what happened."

Vivian White pulled away from the door, rewrapping her arms around her waist, and paced around her cell.

"We was in the yard. Some white bitch kept yappin' about Ghetz, practically singin' about what a motherfuckin' hero he is like he's the second comin' or some shit. It's just like with the guards; the white bitches are whoopin' and laughin' and shoutin' 'amen,' and the black bitches are all scowlin' and shit. Gasoline and matches, Doctor Montgomery. This place is gonna blow apart over that piece of shit, whichever way things come down."

Donovan considered that could well be true, not just the perceived drama in the mind of a troubled young woman. The civil unrest brewing throughout Chicago because of Ghetz was surely happening tenfold inside the jail.

"Okay, Vee, you're in the yard. What happened next?"

Vivian stopped pacing and stared at the door, not quite at Donovan's eyes, which is all she could see, but at the door, lost in some dark reflection.

"I just … I couldn't take it. I just wanted her to shut her mouth. Just shut her mouth. So I doubled my fist and hit her—in the mouth. But then, I don't know … I … kept hittin' her. I must have hit her plenty before they got to me because … because I had an awful lot of blood on me, you know. An awful lot."

The doctor had heard enough.

"Vivian, we're gonna make this right, okay? You trust me, right?"

"Yes, ma'am. Yes, ma'am, I do."

"Well, if they had you off of your meds, that's on them. We can make this situation you're in right now less—punitive by documenting that it was their neglect that put you in that vulnerable position. And we'll get you back on those meds today. I'm going to see about getting you moved to Cermak Hospital next door. They'll be better prepared to treat your situation until we get you back on course. And Vee, don't ever let anybody tell you that you can't or shouldn't talk. That's not true. You can. You should. And you should be able to contact me and talk to me whenever you need to. Don't forget that—*ever.*"

For the first time during that visit, the young woman smiled. "Yes, ma'am."

Donovan nodded and smiled. "You hang tight, Vee."

"Thank you, Doctor Montgomery. Thank you, my angel," she said, more calmly now. Donovan started to turn away, when Vivian said, "I know him, you know."

Donovan froze, then stepped back to the door. "You know Mason Ghetz?"

"He's the sonofabitch who shot Rosie up with that meth. She knew he was dealin,' and she was gonna call him out. Guess it was easier to kill her than keep her quiet." Tears filled the young woman's eyes. "I told the police. They said they was on it, but they didn't do shit. Don't matter too much now anyway, I suppose. Rosie's still dead."

She wiped away the tears before they could fall and shook her head defiantly. "Somebody better put him away permanent-like, Doctor Montgomery, cuz if I ever get the chance, I'm gonna crush that maggot myself."

Donovan took a deep breath, attempting to smile at her patient. She slowly stepped away from the steel door and back down the long hall, eager to conclude her extended visit to 26th and Cal for the day. As she turned the corner, she took out her phone to start the process of getting Vivian moved and back on her meds. To retrieve the number of the Admissions Office at the hospital, she paused, scrolling through her contacts. While doing so, she overheard a conversation coming from the direction of Vivian's cell.

A woman with a low, husky voice was talking quietly but firmly.

"Now, I heard all that shit your doctor friend just spewed at you, and I *know* you know better than that, right? You don't have any rights here, bitch. You only talk when I tell you to. You only breathe when I say you can. And you sure as hell don't get to call on her high-and-mighty ass whenever you feel like it, okay? You ain't worth shit, White. You're in *prison*. And if you keep stirring the pot like you do, you are going to seriously wish you hadn't. Do you understand me? You got no rights. You got no voice. You ain't got shit."

Donovan couldn't believe what she was hearing and aborted her call to confront the woman harassing her patient.

Sidling up to the large matron, she said, "How dare you eavesdrop on my conversation with my patient. How *dare* you. You're working in a correctional institution, and you just broke the law. There is such a thing as doctor/patient confidentiality, Ms. …" She glanced at the woman's name badge. "Ms. Preston. And who do you think you are feeding her all that hogwash about not having any rights? She does have a voice. She does have rights. And you know what you've got? You've got some time on your hands because I'm going to see to it that you can't say shit like that to one more incarcerated soul."

The woman's jaw slacked as she stared at her surprise company. While Donovan called her out, the expression on the matron's face shifted from shock to panic to cold anger, the kind that usually precedes a physical altercation, all in a matter of seconds.

"You think you can fuck with me, doctor-do-good? This here is *my* turf. You're in *my* playground now. So, bring it."

Donovan took a step back and pulled out her phone. "Your *turf*? Are we in a production of *West Side Story*?" she muttered as she called the head of the Board of Trustees, a man she knew both personally and professionally. She gave him a brief but colorful version of what had just transpired as she and the woman locked eyes. Then, "Okay. No, I'm okay. I am. Thank you so much, Tim. I'll let her know that someone is on their way to relieve her for the rest of the day and that the board will be in touch. Thanks again, Tim. Love to Maggie. Okay. Bye-bye."

The woman stood defiant, but Donovan could see that her tough veneer was peeling rapidly. Then Donovan got up close to the woman, kissing close.

"And if you do one more nasty thing to Vivian White, you touch one hair on her head, you even look at her sideways, I promise you—I *promise* you I will have more than your job. I will hunt you down. Then I will drag you out from under whatever dung heap you call home and show you some tough love, okay? And girl, you won't be needing a job after that."

Only two expressions now flashed interchangeably across the large woman's face: bluster to fear, back and forth. She had been rendered speechless by this devastating, swift display of offensive warfare.

Donovan then retreated, calmly throwing out, *"Bring it?* Bitch, please."

Walking through the parking lot to her car, she took care of Vivian's transfer and medications. It was a stunning coincidence, her patient having such a personal past with Mason Ghetz. But as she considered the man and the environment, it seemed possible—even logical—that more than one of the inmates knew the man, either as a victim or cohort.

As she drove back to her office in Lincoln Square, she filed all of that away and turned her attention back to the unsettling conversation she'd had with Ghetz, sifting each comment and nuance for a clue as to what puzzle piece had gotten lost under the rug.

Despite a rocky start, he had eventually answered every question she'd asked. He convincingly regurgitated what she explained to him regarding the purpose of the trial and charges against him. He even acquiesced to recalling the events of October 2nd in detail. Throughout, he maintained that he killed the men in the Walmart parking lot in self-defense, but that was to be expected.

But there was something else, something that had gotten her defenses up, undefined warnings that she couldn't heed because she couldn't read them clearly. The traffic was brutal, which gave her time to think.

After the hour it took to get there, Donovan appreciated the quiet, old-school, high-end glamour that is Lincoln Square even more than usual on that day. She rolled into a parking space in front of the building where she kept her office on the corner of Lawrence and Western. Her townhome on Winnemac was only a few minutes away. She loved every inch of her city, but this was the Chicago she adored.

Brick buildings and even some cobblestones remained in Lincoln Square, a nineteenth-century neighborhood that bustled with coffeehouses, music, art galleries, and on-trend eateries.

As Donovan removed the ignition key, she noticed some mud on the leopard-print floor mat under her kitten-heeled pump. Though the gold-and-black-spotted print gracefully hid a fair amount of grit and grime, this mud was visible. She deduced that it had come back with her from 26th and Cal. Bringing that dirt into this neighborhood wasn't going to work for her, metaphorically or literally.

She exited the car, dragging the mat out as well. Shaking off much of the dirt, she then retrieved a small hard-bristled brush from the back of the gleaming white Prius, and when she was satisfied with her efforts, she replaced the mat and locked the door. Maybe she couldn't yet figure out Mason Ghetz, but she could fix the problem of the dirty floor mat.

Donovan entered the building and took the stairs up to her two-room office on the third floor where she had practiced for the past ten years. Stylish but inviting, the front reception room was dressed with a cozy couch, two matching club chairs, a television on the wall, and enough magazines and flowers to keep even the most agitated patient comfortable while waiting for an appointment. She had made a commitment long ago to maintain a private practice in addition to her forensic work with law enforcement.

There was also a desk in this waiting room, a desk that belonged to her secretary, Angel Torres. Angel kept the doctor's appointments, both in-office and elsewhere, and took care of a million other tasks on a daily basis. Her input, talents, and soothing way with patients made her invaluable to the doctor. And she had been a friend of Donovan's since childhood, which sealed the allegiance between the two women.

The doctor was happy to see that no patients were waiting when she entered the room. Angel jumped up as Donovan walked in. "Hey, girl," she said, then bounded over to the doctor and threw her arms around her. This was not her usual speak or action.

"Whoa, Ange. What's up? You okay?" She held her at arm's length, both women still attached with their hands on each other's elbows.

"I—I'm not over the shooting this morning, I guess," she responded. "Body count went up to thirty-two. Thirty-two people gunned down out of the blue, and, of course, there you were right in the middle of it."

Donovan could see that Angel was genuinely upset about the shooting in Daley Plaza. Everyone was. But she knew this woman, and something else had upset her. The doctor tried to read whatever it was behind her friend's dark eyes, but couldn't.

Changing the subject from one horror to another, Angel asked, "How did your meeting go with the neo-Nazi?" as she moved back toward her desk and Donovan reached for the mail in her inbox.

"It was—interesting. I think the fellow has aspirations of being the next Hannibal Lecter, but he just doesn't have the charm to pull it off."

All at once she stopped riffling through the bills and catalogs. Holding the mail in one hand, she crossed her arms and faced her secretary. "Okay, I give. You want to tell me what's got you so wigged out?"

Giving up the ghost, Angel's mouth opened as if she were about to speak, then closed.

"Angel"—the doctor put down the mail and walked over to her friend— "Angel, I don't remember seeing you like this, honey, and we've known each other for an awfully long time. Just tell me what happened."

"Donovan—I opened the mail earlier."

"And?"

"And this came for you."

She handed the doctor a manila envelope from which Donovan extracted an 8X10 photograph of a lynching. The original photo had been printed in sepia tone and showed the weathering and damage around its edges common in old photos. But this was a replica of the original.

In the photo, three African American men hung limp from three sturdy-looking branches of a large tree, nooses tied around each of their broken necks. Klansmen stood on either side of the hanging bodies wearing the white hooded robes associated with their fraternity.

The headshot of Donovan used on the dust jacket of her new book had been shrunk down, copied, and glued over each of the dead men's faces. The juxtaposition of the doctor's polished headshot atop the three twisted, dangling carcasses was particularly chilling.

No note had been included, and the envelope had no markings.

The two women stood in silence for a long moment. "What do you want me to do?" Angel finally asked.

Donovan stared at the picture then the envelope. "When did this come?"

"I went to pick up a sandwich around two o'clock. I was only gone for about twenty minutes. When I got back, someone had slid it under the door. That was only like two hours ago. Do you think this has something to do with that freak you just interviewed? I mean, what is this even about?"

Donovan considered those words, then put the photo back in the envelope and the envelope under her arm. "Well, it wasn't him. He was tied up at the time. I imagine it means somebody doesn't like my book."

Angel was not amused. "Or somebody wants you dead."

"Maybe. Everybody's a critic." She swooped up the other mail and started for her office, adding, "I'm hoping you've reworked my appointments. I'm going to need some quality time to prep for the trial on Monday. And I'd like your list of all the literary stuff: appearances and interviews, etcetera. I want to check your notes against mine."

"Damn it, Donovan." Donovan stopped and turned toward Angel. "Seriously, what do you want me to do about that photo?"

Donovan could see that Angel was very upset and that her glibness was not getting her out of addressing the situation. Angel deserved a little more sincerity. "There's nothing to be done. I will call the cops when I'm done writing up the Ghetz assessment. It's after four o'clock now, and I want to have it couriered over to Jordan's office this evening."

Her secretary appeared like she was about to cry.

"Angel, this isn't a thing. Remember the three heads in the basement freezer? Now, that was a thing."

She was smiling. Angel was not. "I'm fine. I'm going to stay fine. I promise."

The doctor went into her office and closed the mahogany door behind her. Everything in the room was clean and ordered, lux and lovely. Donovan liked it that way. She always felt better in controlled environments. She could think. She could relax.

Out her third-story window on the pretty street below, she watched a couple grab a kiss while waiting at a crosswalk, and two young men walking a small dog in a loose-knit sweater. Whispering to herself, she said, "Now, this has been quite a day. It surely has. And—it ain't over yet."

She placed the envelope containing the photo of the lynching in the same drawer from which she removed case notes in a file labeled "Mason Ghetz."

Chapter Five

Once Donovan finished the assessment on Ghetz and had it couriered to Jordan's office, she eagerly climbed into the Prius and made her way home. It was after seven o'clock. She hadn't eaten anything all day, but the push to be in her nice, warm townhouse and kick off her shoes trumped the desire to stop in at any of the local eateries for takeout.

Once she entered the picturesque nineteenth-century brick bombshell she called home and made good on her promise to lose the shoes before she closed the front door behind her, her surroundings took on the soft, familiar shimmer of comfort. She extracted her phone from her purse and placed it, along with the envelope holding the photograph of the lynching, on a table next to the black club chair she usually frequented.

The polished hardwood floor felt smooth and sturdy beneath her feet, and the art deco floor lamp near the door cast a soothing, ambient glow. Every time she entered this sanctuary, she felt safe.

The sleek, sophisticated furnishings, along with an enviable collection of African art and cache of colorful throw pillows staged casually around the room, managed to create an earthy vibe, as she had arranged them to do.

After changing into her sweats and vintage Chicago Cubs T-shirt, she lit a stick of Nag Champa, her incense of choice; flipped on a programmed music station that piped in an endless playlist of throbbing, hypnotic techno beats; and turned on the table lamp as she plopped down into that favorite chair.

From here, with her head nestled against the back cushion, she noticed the shoes still on the floor by the front door. There was a time that kicking off and leaving shoes on the floor would have been out of the question for Donovan Montgomery. Intentionally leaving them there was a new game she had devised for herself, designed to gain control over rather developed obsessive-compulsive tendencies. Her hyperfixated impulses to always make sure everything was in its proper place aided in making her an extraordinary profiler and psychiatrist, as she never missed even the most buried bread crumb each case and patient attempted to hide. But in her home, she decided to work on untethering her fixations, even if just a little. Overcoming her compulsions to be in control of every aspect of her surroundings would make her even more in control, she had decided.

As the Nag Champa filled the room and her senses, she reached in the ashtray on the table next to the chair and extracted the glass pot stick perpetually resting there for her occasional indulgence. This particular method of unwinding the day's tensions worked better and more consistently for the doctor than did pills or liquor.

Requiring little time investment and none of the guesswork that hallucinogenics inspired, Donovan knew that not only did the THC in the pot promote less bridled thinking, but if she became relaxed enough, she could commonly access a mental zone located in the deep well of her subconscious mind. There she could see a broader variety of disturbing possibilities, more strategic moves on whatever dangerous chessboard she was currently under contract to play upon. And it was in this altered state that she had harnessed some of her most astounding revelations, those that had taken many bad people off the streets.

Reclined and mind altered, Donovan absorbed the looping rhythms and rich scent of incense to take her into the mind space she wanted to explore. As this wave of focused tranquility washed over her, she carefully slid the photograph out of the envelope and placed it in her lap, her legs folded under her in the large chair.

Something about the figures captured in the picture circulated in her mind. A niggling feeling kept tugging at her that somehow all that had transpired on that day was intertwined: the photograph, the shooting, maybe even Mason Ghetz. But that didn't make sense.

Filing any hypothesized relationship between the three factors, she allowed herself to revisit the details of the shooting in Daley Plaza. She had seen a flash, then another, then a battery of bullets slicing through the crowd.

The state's attorney's bodyguard fell. Donovan toppled Jordan, then Jen Park, and remained there as she watched Maurice Brown finally hit the ground. She saw skateboards rolling unattended in the frozen moment after the bullets and before the panic set in. Screams. People running. People cowering wrapped around one another under benches, near the fountain, beneath the Picasso. The reporter she heard on the radio driving home said that the fifty-foot-tall sculpture had miraculously remained unscathed through the attack. How that was possible escaped Donovan.

She took another pull on the pot stick and closed her eyes, replaying the tape again in her head. She recalled a flash. Then another. Then a battery of flashes.

A dog began barking incessantly from just outside Donovan's bay window. As she opened her eyes and turned toward the sound, she remembered Ghetz barking. She got up and moved to the window, pulling open the bark-cloth drapes.

There stood her neighbor with his dog on a leash, smiling sheepishly and mouthing, "I'm sorry" as his dog fell quiet while urinating on the wall under the window. Another man walking a dog in the opposite direction served as the explanation for the momentary kerfuffle.

Donovan smiled back and returned to the chair and the photo, but now couldn't get Mason Ghetz out of her thoughts. "See you soon," he had said when she was leaving the cell. And he would. He would see her at his trial on Monday. That's what he had meant—the trial. Right? How else? He was being held in a maximum-security prison. She had been threatened before. She had been attacked. Something about Mason Ghetz kept the perpetually balanced doctor unsure of her footing.

Maybe it's that gold-capped tooth gleaming from between those thin purple lips that I find so difficult to tolerate, she thought.

Donovan stared down at the image in her lap. The KKK had been such a devotedly clandestine fraternity. They wore white hooded robes as one way of protecting that anonymity. They hid. Now they didn't. What had changed?

Something had. Something had encouraged these present-day Klansmen to come out of hiding and flip back the hoods of those robes. Every hate organization had gotten bigger, stronger, and more vocal in recent years. The beast had grown while Donovan watched. In this new world, Dracula could walk right in—uninvited.

Donovan took one more hit and stared at the photograph that showed three hanging men, their necks stretched and bent, the doctor's face glued over each of theirs. She whispered, "I'm so sorry they did that to you," to the image in her hands. "Then and now," she added, before once again closing her eyes.

A knock at the door brought her to full consciousness. The barking dog at the window had not been enough to require she completely leave her altered state of mind, but the repeated banging on the door did the trick.

Though she remained pleasantly high, she knew she would not be able to reenter the mental space she had just been pried from—not that evening, anyway.

But even solving the most complex crimes paled in comparison to what awaited her on the other side of the door. There, Alfredo and his husband Mark stood holding takeout from Tom Lee's Chop Suey on North Western and a pint of Ben and Jerry's. "Surprise!" Mark said. Alfredo grinned, holding up the bags of Chinese food.

"How did you know I was famished?" she asked as she opened the door, and the two made their way past her into the room.

"We assumed you would be. We could smell the weed all the way across town," Alfredo quipped. Mark took in a long sniff and exhaled, smiling. "I feel better already," he said, disappearing into the kitchen with the ice cream.

Alfredo stopped to pass off the bags to Donovan, then tripped over the doctor's shoes. He froze. She gave him a toothy smile. "Excellent progress, Doctor Montgomery," he said, scowling at her jokingly while rubbing his ankle.

"Right?" she replied, adding, "Physician, heal thyself" as she placed the bags on the dining room table, flipped off the music, and started removing the various paper containers. "Grab some plates, luv," she called to Mark.

"On it," he called back, reentering the room with a short stack of red Fiestaware and a fistful of serving utensils.

"Hope it's all right that we bullied our way into your home tonight. I had the most horrible thought that you might not have had a moment to eat today," Alfredo said.

"You were born to be a profiler," Donovan responded.

The three friends sat at the table busying themselves with the food, filling their own plates and each other's as they chatted.

"God, Donovan, I never get over this place. It's too fabulous," Mark gushed. "Hollywood gorgeous, but still so warm and—I don't know—lived in." Alfredo nodded in agreement. "Why are you so cool again?" Mark asked playfully.

"Well, if my dad hadn't left this to me when he died, I couldn't afford to be quite this cool, Mark," Donovan reminded him. "Besides, it's not like I own the whole building, just this floor."

"Poor little thing," he said, shaking his head and plucking a shrimp from her plate with his chopsticks. "Just the one floor."

As second helpings were dished, the idle chitchat turned more substantive with the mass shooting becoming the focus. Alfredo confirmed what Angel had reported to Donovan earlier, that, indeed, thirty-two people had died that morning in Daley Plaza. Yes, Alfredo was in the process of seeing them all. No, the cops still had no leads.

"How about, you, Doctor? What are your thoughts? After all, you were right in the center of it." Alfredo genuinely wanted to know Donovan's take on what might have happened but hadn't quite put to bed the fact that his closest pal had, once again, been an arm's throw from death.

Donovan swallowed while considering her words. "The shooter or shooters couldn't have been at street level. I'd say the gunfire came from the Chicago Temple Building."

Alfredo wiped his mouth with a paper napkin and placed it next to his plate. "Okay. Why not another building across the street?"

Donovan looked squarely at him, and with calm certainty said, "Because the bullets didn't hit the Picasso. What was being targeted was to the right of the sculpture, clearing it. The focus was on a particular spot. It was made to appear like a random shooting, but it wasn't. It wasn't random, Alfredo. I think Jen was the target."

Doctor Ramos placed his hand over his husband's on the table. "You could be right. I don't know. But I've got thirty-two people on slabs in the morgue who would deeply appreciate an answer."

The three got up simultaneously. Mark started to clear the table. "Don't even think about it," Donovan said, stacking plates and gathering utensils.

"All right, my beautiful weirdo. May I put the leftovers in the fridge?"

"That would be lovely," she said with a smile.

Mark closed the paper containers and placed them in the refrigerator. Donovan spent a couple minutes more getting her kitchen in order and a pot of coffee brewing to accompany the ice cream. When she reentered the front room, both men were standing by the club chair on which she had left the photograph of the lynching.

Alfredo held the photo. Mark's hands were in the prayer position, pressed against his mouth. "Was this delivered to you here?" Alfredo asked, assessing that the doctored photo had come to his friend in the manila envelope on the table.

Donovan sauntered toward the men, her arms crossed. "No. It came to the office. Angel had stepped out when it was dropped off. She was really shaken by it. I don't think I've ever seen her so upset."

Alfredo threw the photo back on the chair. "Really? She found a photograph of a lynching with Klansmen next to some hanging bodies and your face all over it to be upsetting? That's odd."

The three stood together near the chair. "Were you going to tell me?"

"Sure."

"After the ice cream?"

"Alfredo …"

"Did you at least tell the cops? They need to check for prints."

"I was going to tonight. I—I just wanted to … Anyway, odds are against finding a print, but I've been careful with it, just in case." She picked up the photograph and slid it into the envelope, placing it on the table.

Mark wrapped his arms around her. After a second of leaving her arms at her sides, she hugged him back. "What the fuck?" he whispered.

The three sat down in silence, Donovan in her club chair, the couple on the couch. Alfredo leaned forward, legs apart, elbows on knees, thinking. "Donovan, is it possible that this could be some kind of publicity stunt?"

Both Mark and Donovan jumped to full attention when Alfredo posed the question. "Oh my God, Alfie," Donovan exclaimed.

"I just thought I'd ask. Publishers are ruthless when it comes to marketing their clients. That thing would garner a lot of press. It's hard to sell books these days," he said.

"Not mine," she responded.

"What about the neo-Nazi?" he countered.

"How? The timing is off. He didn't even know who was showing up to perform the assessment today."

"Why didn't he know?" Alfredo asked.

Donovan leaned forward, legs spread, elbows on knees, mirroring Alfredo. "I don't know. But he seemed surprised when I showed up. Why would that be?"

The street-facing bay window exploded with a sound like a bomb going off, spraying glass into the living room. Donovan, Alfredo, and Mark instinctively covered their heads. When it was clear that this wasn't gunfire or an actual bomb, Donovan was the first to move. She ran to the window in the hopes of catching some glimpse of the assailant, but there was no sign of anyone anywhere. Whoever threw the brick had gotten away quickly, most likely in a car.

"Are you two all right?" she asked, still checking the quiet street.

After taking a moment to be sure he was all right, Mark said, "Yes. Are you okay?"

They then turned their attention to the red clay culprit lying on the hardwood floor. It had landed near the table where they had just finished their meal. Glass from the window had pelted the dining area like glistening confetti. No note was attached to the brick. There didn't need to be. The message was clear. The doctor was to back off her testimony scheduled for the trial of Mason Ghetz.

"Yeah, I'm fine."

Alfredo got out his phone and called the cops. While he relayed the evening's festivities to the person on the other end of the call, Mark addressed the doctor, first turning her shoulders so that she was facing him directly. "Come stay with us, honey. You'll be safer at our place. At least until the trial is over."

She thought for a moment, but they both knew the answer. She had always felt so safe in her home, and she was never, ever willing to let the bad guys win.

She gently squeezed Mark's arm. "Thank you, luv. I'm staying right here. Look, that photo and brick may not be the end of the harassment before I testify. There have been plenty of other creeps over the years who have used similar scare tactics in an effort to keep me from talking. It's never worked, and it's not going to now."

Alfredo put his phone away and joined the conversation. "They're on their way. I agree with Mark. Come stay with us."

"I'm staying here, Alfie."

"Of course you are. Then let me have a cop assigned to you until after the trial."

"I'll be fine," she said, but the men could see that she was considering that option. She had seen much over the years, but something about this case had felt different from the beginning.

Alfredo bowed his head to meet her gaze. "Well, I respect your opinion, Doctor. I just don't want to see you on my table."

They watched as a squad car double-parked in front of the townhouse. "God, that was fast," Mark said.

Alfredo again regarded Donovan, who knew he was waiting for an answer.

"Okay," she said. "Just until the trial is over."

Chapter Six

There was a media circus in front of the Criminal Courthouse at 26th and Cal that Monday morning. Cars belched out onto the street. The lot was full. Police stood sentinel all around the periphery of the old building.

Camera crews perched side by side like pigeons on the lip of the fountain that divided the Courthouse and Administration Building. News vans were scattered across the dead lawn, each marking territory among the barren trees that freckled the landscape between California Avenue and the courthouse steps. Everybody wanted to get as close as possible to the action, whatever that action was going to be.

Mason Ghetz was big news, and though the trial itself held more complicated subtleties regarding self-defense and reasonable doubt, the clear line that the case had drawn societally was undeniably black and white.

One of the less-publicized congressional candidates seized the opportunity to grab a moment of invaluable television coverage, saying, "Mason Ghetz was defending himself, pure and simple. He is being railroaded like so many other innocent victims of black racism. And that is clearly what this is: black racism. Make no mistake, my friends, the white race is under attack, and this bogus witch hunt of a trial is just one more opportunity for that hatred to rear its ugly head."

As Donovan and the cop that Alfredo had assigned to accompany her passed that particular candidate on their way to the building, a half-dozen microphones were pointed at him like foils in a fencing match. She thought how extraordinary it was that he would say those sentiments aloud and that his remarks would undoubtedly get a huge amount of media attention for at least a day. And she knew that despite or because of his sensational opinions, he would remain, to some degree, a viable option for a seat in Congress because there were people who agreed with him one hundred percent. Many people.

Before ascending the steps to the building, she glanced over her shoulder. Collected to one side, an all-white crowd stood rigid. Many wore T-shirts with "Make America Great Again" and "White and Proud" silkscreened across their chests. She caught the eye of one such protester sporting a swastika tattoo on his forehead. His icy gaze would have unnerved anyone except the woman he had just aimed it at.

To the other side stood a collection of black, white, and brown protesters bouncing pasteboard signs in the air and chanting slogans such as "Racism IS NOT Patriotism" and "Hate is Anti-GOD." The signs were glued to wooden stakes. Donovan noticed that several of those stakes had been chiseled to points and that the wood extending past the sign was visible.

Whether this weaponization was meant as a threat or defense was unclear. What came across with crystal clarity was the optic. Images of Charlottesville ran through Donovan's memory as she turned away and entered the courthouse.

The lobby of the historic courthouse where so many famous cases had been tried, from Al Capone to R. Kelly, continued to serve as a formidable ambassador for a building where much had fallen into disrepair. Some parts of the courthouse were severely dog-eared and less than polished, but the 1920s architecture and appointments of the lobby, from the grand pillars to brass fixtures, remained impressive.

On that day, the imposing foyer was packed to capacity. Though many racially charged trials had taken place at the Cook County Criminal Courthouse, none had inspired the physical presence of so many people as did the trial of Mason Ghetz.

The neo-Nazi's well-documented relationship with the Aryan Brotherhood and long list of crimes for which he had been charged and convicted did not alter the fact that at that moment, his guilt or innocence had yet to be determined. Of course, as Jordan pointed out, it would be hard to make a strong case for self-defense in favor of someone who shot people in the back of their heads as they ran. Odds were good that the trial, no matter how salacious, would be a short one.

Donovan and her escort parted ways as she was ushered into the prep room where State's Attorney Jordan Payne stood over a table full of file boxes. Jordan's two assistants were also present, along with a clerk. In case a gofer was needed for anything, the clerk would take care of whatever it was so that neither assistant would be compelled to leave Jordan's side and could remain at his beck and call, as was usually necessary in any high-profile case.

"Morning, Doctor Montgomery. How are you this fine day?" Jordan asked, barely glancing up from the files he was sorting and passing to one of his assistants.

Donovan nodded at the other three in the room while she removed her coat. She then placed it over the back of a chair, setting her clutch purse on the seat. "Morning. Quite a zoo out there, Counselor. How's it going in here?"

"Super fantastic," Jordan said sarcastically, then stopped what he was doing and looked up at the doctor. "Hey, did you receive any more threats since the brick incident?"

She shook her head no. "I've had a string of phone calls. Nobody speaks. They just hang up as soon as I say hello. Other than that, nothing to report."

"So, they have your cell number," he said. She nodded affirmatively. "Nice. Let me guess. All restricted numbers, right? No way to trace 'em?" he asked. Again, she nodded yes. "Perfect."

Just then Jordan's cell phone vibrated loudly from his jacket pocket. After removing it and glancing at the name displayed, he said, "Shit. Donovan, please take a seat. This is going to take a minute, I'm afraid."

She smiled calmly and sat in a chair against the wall, absorbing the familiar decay of her surroundings. None of the chairs matched. The cushions on the few that had them were flat and frayed. Pipes and radiators hissed audibly through yellowed walls, and the room threw off the faint scent of ammonia and sweat. The elongated table on which Jordan and his team were preparing their paperwork had long ago fallen victim to the opinions of others, their anger and frustration carved into its surface with sharp objects and ballpoint pens.

A moderate amount of natural light made its way into the room. Donovan got up and peeked out a window, downtown visible in one direction, buildings wrapped in barbed wire visible in the other.

"May I have the clerk get you a cup of coffee, Doctor Montgomery?" asked one of Jordan's assistants.

Donovan turned away from the window and faced the young professional who already had too many lines on her face for a woman of her age. "Oh, no thanks," she responded.

Beyond the assistant, Donovan could see Jordan slipping his phone back to the inside pocket of his suit jacket. He hailed her over to the long table where they each took a seat, as did both assistants and the clerk. They discussed briefly what the doctor would be covering on the stand, making sure no stone would be left unturned in her testimony.

"You understand that the roof is going to come off of that courtroom when you give your testimony, right?" Jordan said to Donovan.

"I do suppose that is to be expected, Counselor. Nevertheless, it is what it is. I stand behind my findings and my assessment of those findings." The two sat staring into one another's eyes. Donovan could see that Jordan needed more convincing. "Hey—Jordan, you know that I've given all of the facts every consideration," she added. "You *know* that I have."

Jordan finally nodded. Though he was concerned about her testimony, he had never been the slightest bit concerned about the doctor's unflagging commitment to her work.

The door opened and a guard appeared. "The trial is about to begin," he said to everyone in the room.

Both assistants and the clerk conferred quietly while gathering files and exiting the room in tandem. Donovan got up and pushed in her chair. Jordan stood and folded his hands in front of him to address his star witness. "Are you ready, Doctor?"

"I am," she answered sweetly, stoically.

The two were now alone in the room. "That call I just took was someone from Jen's office. He said the courtroom is SRO. He's guessing there are over a hundred people stuffed in there and probably another thousand outside trying to get in. The cops are keeping the hallway in front of the courtroom tightly monitored, though, so you won't have to sign too many autographs while you're waiting."

She cocked her head and grinned. He grinned back.

"Alfredo is going to testify first, followed by Detective DuMont, so you have a little time on your hands right now, okay?" he asked.

"Okay," she answered.

"Look, I have nothing but confidence in you, Donovan Montgomery. Besides, this thing should be a slam-dunk. Both sides want it wrapped up ASAP." He leaned toward her but kept his hands folded together. "Let's do this," he said, then extended an arm to guide her out of the room ahead of him. She picked up her clutch, leaving her coat, and slid past him into the hall.

Cook County's lead medical examiner, Doctor Alfredo Ramos, reported his findings to the jury, explaining the entrances and exits of the bullets that killed the three black men and wounded another attempting to flee from a Walmart parking lot on the night in question.

He answered a battery of other forensic questions from Jordan and was then only briefly cross-examined by Defense Counsel Bell Dean, a formidable presence in many other high-profile cases, and nearly all high-profile cases that involved any racial divides.

With her soft Southern drawl and thick snow-white hair that she kept ratted and sprayed, she had become the popular choice among Caucasians, whether the accused was an active member of the Aryan Brotherhood or any other white person suspected of doing anything to anyone of any other color. She didn't come cheap, so it was likely someone other than Ghetz had footed her bill. That was curious.

Knowing she had some time on her hands, Donovan decided on that cup of coffee after all and took a detour from her jaunt to the courtroom to visit the café. While paying the cashier, she became aware of being watched. Without lifting her head from the task at hand, she finished, put her change in her wallet, then turned. Two men with shaved heads were standing by the entrance, both staring at her, neither speaking.

She left the café without any confrontation, though she could feel their eyes remain on her until she moved out of their sightline. Deciding that it might be best to position herself near the courtroom where she would soon be needed, she kept walking.

As she made her way down each corridor, her heels clicked against the scuffed white linoleum that covered the majority of the floor, a pattern of black flecks running throughout each tile. She thought how those flecks kept the flooring from seeming as battered as it was.

Donovan made her way to the courtroom just as Alfredo was leaving it. The two friends nodded and smiled. Both kept moving. On the bench next to the doors sat Detective James DuMont, who was being called in as Alfredo left. When Detective DuMont rose to go in, he and Donovan nodded to one another as well.

The detective moved in close enough to Donovan to whisper something in her ear. "You watch yourself. Guards or no guards, this place is a powder keg right now."

The gesture seemed vaguely paternal, though Donovan couldn't accept that it was, not coming from this man.

She nodded and started to sit down on the bench he had been sitting on. But he wasn't sure that he had made himself clear, reaching out and grabbing the sleeve of her suit jacket. She stopped and gave him her full attention.

"I know you think you're invincible. Sometimes I'm not so sure you're wrong. But I'd hate to have one of these assholes take you down right in the middle of a fucking courthouse. They'd really get a kick out of that. You know they would." He paused to breathe, then softened his delivery a little. "Anybody takes you down, it should be me—the right way." He tried to smile but couldn't quite manage it. "Just watch your back, okay?"

"They're waiting for you, Detective," she responded curtly while a guard held open the door to the courtroom for the detective to enter. He wouldn't budge, continuing to stare at her, his hand still on her arm. Astoundingly, she realized that the man was truly concerned for her safety. All at once, every dark possibility came into focus and she answered him sincerely. "I will, Detective. I promise you, I will."

After a moment of assessment, he nodded, releasing her and removing his hat before entering the courtroom to testify.

Donovan finally sat down on the bench as she considered the detective's adamant warning. A small group of uniformed officers chatted quietly with one another directly in front of her. Three men stood to the right of those officers. Like the men in the café, their heads were shaved clean. She could see that one of them had a tattoo on his neck, but she couldn't make out what it was a tattoo of. It appeared to be a symbol of some kind.

The men stopped talking and scowled at her as soon as she sat down. She glanced at them for a moment, then looked straight ahead into nothingness. A few seconds passed before the hissing began. The sound was low at first then grew louder until she, once again, gazed in their direction. One of the three men was hissing like a snake and staring right at her—hissing, just as Mason Ghetz had done during the assessment.

When the hissing became annoying to one of the cops who was trying to have a quiet chat with his coworkers, the officer asked the man to keep it down. He reminded the guy that there were trials going on and that if he didn't stop hissing, they would have him removed.

The man stopped hissing. Then, addressing his pals in a voice loud enough for Donovan to hear, he said, "Definitely time we had ourselves a barbecue, fellas. I'm gettin' hungry just thinking about slaughtering that pig and gettin' her ass up on that spit over one o' them good-smellin' fire pits. Shit!" The three grinned, nodding in Donovan's direction.

One of the officers close enough to have caught some of that soliloquy said, "Excuse me? What did you say?" She thought she may have misinterpreted the pig reference. Then she noticed that the hissing man had been looking Donovan's way and said, "Ma'am, is this man bothering you?"

"No," the doctor answered. The officer didn't seem to approve of Donovan's answer. She turned back to the formerly hissing man and said, "Keep it down, okay? Just keep to yourself."

The skinhead made a quick combative gesture as if he might pounce, and all three police officers immediately placed their hands next to their weapons, ready to draw. The three hairless men laughed again.

The policewoman who had spoken to the hisser said, "If you pull a stunt like that again, you'll be asked to leave. And when I say you'll be *asked* to leave, I mean I will drag the three of you clowns off of this floor and directly into a cell. Do you read me, gentlemen?"

"We can't read," one of the men said. This provoked another round of laughter between them as two of the three turned and left. The formerly hissing man remained a second after the others. He turned away from the cops and again toward Donovan, who was watching this entire floor show with great interest.

He forked his fingers and pointed them first at his own eyes, then at the doctor. Back again to his eyes, then back to her. "I'm watching you," was the pantomimed message he left her with before joining his pals.

Shortly after the three hairless men left, so did the cops, and for a handful of minutes, Donovan sat alone on the bench outside of the courtroom, alone but for a guard who paced idly nearby.

When the door to the courtroom opened and Detective DuMont came out, Donovan heard her name called to give her testimony. Once again the detective and doctor passed one another. This time the two shared eye contact only as DuMont replaced his hat and buttoned his coat.

Things have to be a little safer in there, she thought as she entered the rugged old courtroom. The faded oxblood chairs with the dark wood frames that made up the jury box were filled with a collection of twelve pensive people. Donovan observed that more than one of them looked scared. None appeared bored or apathetic, which was sometimes the case with a jury.

Waves of delighted twitters filled the courtroom when Donovan came into view. Many in the audience strained their necks to see around the heads in front of them to watch her walk to the witness stand.

She was a celebrity, after all. Not as important as a reality star or rapper, but most of the people there had seen her on television, and that made her quite noteworthy. America loved its celebrities for however long they could stretch out that fifteen minutes of fame.

At least one person in the room had read her new book. Donovan assumed this because the woman was sitting at the end of a pew holding a copy. It then occurred to Donovan that just because the woman was holding the book didn't mean she had any intention of reading it.

As she made her way to the witness stand, the doctor flashed on various ways that the woman might try to get her to sign it. During her testifying? Maybe chase her out of the courtroom when her testimony concluded? Time would tell.

Donovan Montgomery stood in front of the capacity crowd in the courtroom comprised of skinheads, celebrity junkies, and the families of the deceased men. She stood in front of the judge, jury, and killer as the bailiff swore her in.

Chapter Seven

Wearing a sapphire blue skirt and jacket tailored for impact, as well as a pair of shiny black Jimmy Choos, Donovan Montgomery took the witness stand. Her title, years of experience, and credentials were established for the court. Though typical court protocol was followed, the presiding Judge Robert Hallstrom was already quite familiar with Doctor Montgomery, as she had been a professional witness in his courtroom on more than one occasion. And Donovan knew this judge to be even-handed in his rulings.

The old oxblood leather chairs in the jury box were filled with an ethnically diverse collection of wide-eyed jurors, and all of those eyes were glued to Donovan. A quick check of their body language told the doctor they were all—so far—in complete agreement with her despite the fact that she hadn't said anything yet.

Bell Dean and Donovan made eye contact. Dean had a conservative smile on her face, eyebrows slightly raised and chin tilted upward a little, offering Donovan the same expression one might give a Girl Scout right before she leaps into a fund-raiser sales pitch—kind and condescending.

Mason Ghetz was smiling at Donovan too. But his chin was not tilted upward; it was tilted down.

Once the formalities were out of the way, Jordan Payne asked Donovan to explain Mason Ghetz's family history, which included a father with undiagnosed psychopathy but whose behavior suggested its influence on the young Ghetz, as did his mother's many suicide attempts. Anger and depression were two strong influences that played in the rearing of their only child. Ghetz's early addictions to narcotics and alcohol were also discussed at length.

"Do you assert that these things played into the Walmart parking lot shootings? I mean, just because a person has an unfortunate history of mental illness in the family—even if the person is an addict—that person might well try to defend himself if being attacked. That's not a far-fetched notion, is it, Doctor Montgomery?"

Jordan Payne was in his element and eager to play every chip he had on this hand. Donovan reflected that it had been a long time since she had seen him in action. She was immediately reminded of his polish and intelligence, and that it seemed he had watched a great many Perry Mason episodes as a young man.

"No, that's not far-fetched at all. But this was clearly not an act of self-defense."

"And that conclusion is based on what?"

"Many things. But the trajectory of the bullets is fundamental to both Doctor Ramos's and my findings."

"You mean that Henry Wilson, Bartholomew King, and Peter Darnell could not have been attacking Mr. Ghetz because the bullets went in the back of their heads."

"That's right."

"And that Tommy Parkland, who was in the car assumedly to drive his friends away from this drug deal gone wrong, was not attacking Mr. Ghetz either?"

"Correct."

Then addressing the jury, Jordan Payne added, "As was mentioned briefly earlier today, Mr. Parkland passed away this morning at John H. Stroger Hospital from complications. He had been in a coma brought on by that shooting."

Turning back to Donovan, he asked, "Was there any defect that might have kept the accused from being able to determine what is right and what is wrong? Medications, perhaps, that might have altered or clouded his judgment?"

"Mr. Ghetz has an ongoing relationship with alcohol and street narcotics. His appetites color all of his activities. They do not, however, direct them."

"How do you mean?"

"Maybe he had a drink. Maybe he popped a pill. It is my assertion that he would have shot those men regardless."

"So, let me have you restate for the jury what we have established. Do you believe that Mason Ghetz was suffering from a mental illness that would have led him to shoot those men?"

"No, I do not."

"Is it your opinion that Mason Ghetz is not guilty by reason of insanity?"

"Based on my evaluation, it is my professional medical opinion that on the night in question, Mr. Ghetz was not suffering from a mental illness at the time of the offense that would have provoked and/or primarily influenced the shootings, that he understood what he was engaging in, and therefore had the capacity to know and understand the potential consequences of his actions. It is my expert medical opinion that Mr. Ghetz did not suffer from a mental illness that would have impaired his ability to understand the nature, quality, and wrongfulness of his actions. There is an application used in forensic psychiatry that originated in the 1840s called the M'Naghten Rule. It's an assessment specifically designed to determine whether the person accused of a crime was sane at the time of the crime. It determines whether the accused should be held criminally responsible for the wrongdoing. This is how we gauge criminal insanity."

"Is he then, in your medical opinion, also competent to stand trial and understand the proceedings of his case?"

"Yes," Donovan replied immediately. "Mr. Ghetz has the ability to understand these proceedings, which I have noted in my report. My report and conclusions are based on the review of myriad interviews and various documents, including his medical, psychosocial, employment, and educational background."

"Having gathered what you assert to be pertinent records and documents and other relevant information along with your professional evaluation, have you, therefore, determined that Mason Ghetz shot those men in self-defense? Or was it murder, Doctor Montgomery?"

Being a physician retained to answer medico-legal questions, Donovan was familiar with this part of the game. She could give Jordan Payne a nuanced answer. Leaving wiggle room would make her position less easily disputed and more readily accepted by the court. But she chose, instead, to push the envelope and common professional stance. "It was murder."

The crowd twittered softly. Bell Dean shook her head and lifted her hands a few inches off the table in an "Oh brother" sort of way. Donovan was intrigued that she had not objected but knew she was saving up her strength for a brisk cross-examination.

"What is your assessment of future risk here, Doctor?"

"Given a similar scenario, the risk of Mason Ghetz killing again is extremely high. His motivation would be the same."

Jordan placed his hands on the rough dark wood that surrounded the witness stand. He took a moment before asking Donovan the next question. He and the doctor knew what was coming. No one else in the room did. And she could see in his eyes that he was tightening his stomach for the inevitable boxing match that was about to begin.

"And what exactly would that scenario be?"

Donovan coaxed her long hair behind her ear with one index finger while unmooring the single onyx button from its buttonhole on her jacket with the other.

"Any situation wherein he finds himself sexually attracted to someone he deems inappropriate or unacceptable by his own conflicting standards."

The entire congregation seemed to gasp, sucking the oxygen from the room. This was followed by an eruption of chatter from the audience, coinciding with Bell Dean leaping to her feet and loudly addressing Judge Hallstrom.

"Objection, Your Honor! Defense has been the very soul of patience while this allegedly 'professional witness' blathered on about her 'assessments,' but wherever she thinks she's going with this line of skewed deduction is beyond our endurance."

Judge Hallstrom lightly tapped his gavel against its block. "Order," he said softly. The judge then turned to Jordan, who was already addressing the bench.

"Your Honor," Jordan rejoined, "Doctor Montgomery is recognized for being an outstanding professional witness. I believe it would be in this court's best interests to hear her conclusions."

The judge looked to Donovan. "Are you certain that this tack is relevant, Doctor Montgomery?" he asked.

"It is, Your Honor."

"Judge Hallstrom … ," Bell Dean began but was usurped by the judge.

"The doctor's input is welcomed by this court, Ms. Dean. Overruled. Please be seated."

Dean's face went hard as she reseated herself next to Ghetz, who looked like he had heard a fire alarm but was waiting for instruction as to the safest place to run.

Counsel readdressed Donovan. "Doctor Montgomery, are you saying that Mason Ghetz killed those men because he was sexually attracted to one or all of them?"

She took a moment before answering, "Yes."

The volume of chatter escalated to disruptive. Ghetz filled the room with his version of a belly laugh. Dean pleaded with the judge, "Your Honor …"

This time Hallstrom banged his gavel against its block aggressively. "Order. Hush up." Turning immediately to Donovan, he added, "Doctor, whatever this is you're sharing, let's get it expressed as quickly as possible."

"Thank you, Your Honor," Jordan said. Stepping toward Donovan, he asked, "Can you walk us through how Mason Ghetz's sexuality would or could play any factor in the deaths of these four young men, Doctor Montgomery?"

"The documented last words of the driver Tommy Parkland, the young man mortally wounded that night, were, 'That creep is fucked up.' He then repeated the name of one of the other young men, Peter Darnell. He repeated it twice before slipping into a coma from which he did not return."

"Yes, Detective DuMont gave us that information earlier this morning," Jordan confirmed.

Donovan continued. "Peter Darnell had just turned twenty-one the night before the shootings. He had celebrated with his friends. These were a different collection of friends than the ones he was with in the Walmart parking lot. He kept his friends separate, the thugs and the queers."

"Thugs and queers, Doctor?"

"Those were the words Peter used to describe his two lives. According to the friends who were with him on his birthday, Peter had never been to a nightclub. So they took him to Jeffery Pub in Boystown to ring in his twenty-first year. Peter Darnell was gay."

A large woman seated between two other women, all three wearing T-shirts with a photograph of Peter Darnell silkscreened on the front, jumped up, screaming, "How dare you talk about my baby like that! How dare you disgrace my poor baby in this courtroom! He didn't deserve any of this shit! You gonna go to hell for spreading vicious lies!"

Cameras clicked belonging to the news photographers allowed in, and the tone of the courtroom had morphed into something close to chaos. Judge Hallstrom banged his gavel, attempting to steady the proceedings.

"Order! Order! Bailiff, get Mrs. Darnell some water. Mrs. Darnell, please take your seat. Doctor, continue."

"The drug exchange that took place the night of the shootings was not the first time Peter and his thug friends, to use his terminology, had dealt with Mason Ghetz. According to the two gay men who accompanied Peter to Jeffery Pub, he had confided in them on more than one occasion that Mr. Ghetz liked him, that they had much in common as he, too, lived two lives. Ghetz exchanged drugs for sex with Peter."

Ghetz jumped up. And though he was handcuffed and shackled, when he leaped to his feet, every guard in the room turned toward him with hands on their weapons. Cameras continued to click, sounding like a backyard full of crickets as the titillated, panicked symphony of the crowd crescendoed.

"Shut up! Shut the fuck up or I—" His shouts were interrupted by Bell Dean, who jumped up at the same moment to stop one more word from coming out of her client's incriminating mouth. She threw her arms around him to shock and steady him as she whispered something in his ear. Whatever she said made Ghetz relax. After a moment of staring at Dean, he even smiled as he sat back down. Dean then turned back to the bench.

"Objection, Your Honor. How is any of this distasteful, hurtful supposition relevant?" she queried.

"Are we closing in on the big picture, Doctor? Do you promise me relevance? Soon?" asked Judge Hallstrom of Donovan.

"You have my word," she answered.

Jordan once again took to the helm of the questioning. "Are you asserting that Mason Ghetz is gay and that his sexual orientation somehow provoked the shootings?"

Donovan studied the jury. A quick assessment of their body language suggested that they were now divided in their allegiance. She watched the two women sitting to either side of a sobbing Mrs. Darnell escort her out of the courtroom, inspiring another wave of snapshots.

"His sexuality has always been repressed. Ghetz was raised in a home that was filled with distrust and a suffocating lack of respect for other cultures—especially African Americans—and the young Ghetz was forced to hide his penchant for black men. My background on him uncovered one incident in fifth grade wherein he and a black schoolmate were expelled for being discovered in the school bathroom—"

"You're dead, bitch," Ghetz said audibly but calmly. Dean squeezed his hand, whispered to him again, then rose.

"Objection. This is just a ploy to humiliate Mr. Ghetz and divert the jury from the matter at hand! Whatever Mr. Ghetz did or didn't do when he was ten cannot be relevant to who he is today or this trial. This is outrageous!"

Jordan Payne again asked the court's permission to continue.

The judge skeptically granted that permission. "Overruled, Ms. Dean. I understand your concerns, but I want to hear this testimony. Doctor Montgomery may be about to tell this court something it needs to hear. If not, her credibility and reputation will suffer the consequences. And if I hear another outburst from you, Mr. Ghetz, I will hold you in contempt. Is that understood?"

Jordan then turned his attention back to Donovan and asked her to continue.

"It is on record that Mr. Ghetz had an African American teacher in his first year of high school, a young English teacher named Bryce Howard. Mr. Ghetz spent a few afternoons being tutored by Mr. Howard. That summer, Mr. Howard came up missing and was never heard from again. That is the same summer that Mr. Ghetz became a member of the Aryan Brotherhood. It is my professional opinion that Mr. Ghetz buried his inclinations and submerged his lust into hate, most especially toward African American men. His criminal record has confirmed that hatred through a long list of offenses for which he has been charged and convicted over the years."

With his hands clasped behind him, Jordan walked slowly past the jury box and asked, "So, tell this court, Doctor Montgomery, what happened that night in the parking lot?"

Donovan sat up a little straighter, sliding the onyx button back through the buttonhole of her tailored jacket.

"I assert that on the night of the shootings, Tommy Parkland, Henry Wilson, and Bartholomew King saw a side of Ghetz they had not seen before, that he belittled Peter in front of them and forced him to perform a sexual act, which panicked the two young men and the driver, Tommy Parkland. Perhaps he had them all on their knees at gunpoint before each ran and were shot in the back of the head. That will remain a mystery. But what we know is that Peter was gay and hiding that fact, Mason is gay and hiding that fact, that Tommy's last words were, 'That creep is fucked up. Peter. Peter,' and that everyone there that night except for Ghetz is now, as of today, dead.

"It is my medical opinion that Mason Ghetz killed Peter Darnell because he was sexually attracted to him and that he killed the other three men because they could have exposed his motive and sexual orientation. And I believe that he had every intention of the scene going down exactly as he had it planned, with the exception of Tommy Parkland surviving long enough to speak."

"Thank you, Doctor. Nothing further, Your Honor," Jordan said.

"Defense may cross-examine the witness," said Judge Hallstrom.

Attorney Bell Dean stood, shaking out one of the cuffs of her chiffon dress while making her way around the table. She crossed her arms and made eye contact with the jury. "Well, well, well, Doctor Montgomery, that was the single most provocative testimony I have ever heard," she began. "Closer to science fiction than anything based on facts, I'd say."

"Objection, Your Honor," Jordan said.

Dean looked at Jordan and then the judge. "I am confident that I will be able to express myself without objection from counsel, as all of my logical, measured objections have fallen on deaf ears for some reason."

Judge Hallstrom cleared his throat. "Are you questioning my rulings, Counselor?" he asked with a notable dash of indignation in his voice.

Bell Dean allowed her jaw to drop and eyes to widen. "Certainly not, Your Honor. My goodness, no. I have every confidence that you had your reasons. I know without question that I will be given the same considerations as my esteemed colleague. Besides, this won't take but a minute."

"Overruled, Mr. Payne," Judge Hallstrom said, rubbing his eyes behind his glasses. Jordan sat down, crossed his long legs and arms, and waited.

Dean planted herself directly in front of Donovan. "Doctor Montgomery, you have served as a professional witness on a great many trials, so I know that you understand the term 'contextual bias,' is that right?"

Donovan fought to not furrow her brow. "Yes, Counselor, I do."

"Of course you do. For our jury members, I'll explain that contextual bias is when a professional witness, a forensic scientist or doctor or anybody, is unconsciously swayed by irrelevant details wrapped around a case or the accused, and without being aware of it their professional interpretations and assessments are formed by those details, making their findings, unfortunately, not terribly professional. Now, in the—"

Donovan interjected, "I assure you, Counselor, my assertions and assessments were not skewed by any such biases. Mr. Ghetz's pathology is well documented. I stand by my findings."

"That's wonderful! That's wonderful news, Doctor Montgomery. Because you being an African American and Mason Ghetz being a proud member of the White Nationalist Party might get in the way of a lesser professional.

Might color their perspective. I'm delighted that race has played no hand in your summation about what happened that night. We can trust, therefore, that your evaluations were based on heightened deductive reasoning and not some lascivious smear campaign aimed at clouding the jury's heads."

Donovan had an instinct to cross her legs. She did not follow that instinct. She sat up straight and kept a neutral expression on her face.

"Before I let you skedaddle, I would just love to have you confirm for us how intimately familiar you are with what is and is not admissible evidence."

"Quite familiar."

"Again, for the sake of the jury"—she turned from Donovan and toward the jury box—"some evidence is admissible, but some evidence is inadmissible. Inadmissible evidence is when the underlying data behind that evidence is flawed or less than factual. If the data is flawed, then the evidence cannot be taken into account by a jury. As you can imagine, what is admissible and what is inadmissible becomes extremely important in a trial where someone's life is hanging in the balance."

Dean turned back to face Donovan.

"Do you have any questions for me, Counselor?" Donovan asked dryly.

"No, ma'am. I have *nothing* to say to you."

With that, Dean returned to the seat next to Ghetz. Judge Hallstrom told Donovan that she could step down, then addressed the courtroom. "Thank you, Doctor Montgomery. You are free to go. The court will take a recess for lunch. We will resume at one thirty."

Chapter Eight

The following day, with her testimony behind her, Donovan was able to see several of her patients. The waiting room had been full when she arrived at her office that morning. Now, the final patient of the day sat in one overstuffed chair and the doctor in the other.

"Wow. Well, that is quite a nightmare, Ben. Before I give you my take, do you have any ideas about what it might have meant?"

While the man was formulating his response, the door to the doctor's inner office opened. It was Angel. The look on her face was one of fear. Maybe the patient didn't notice, but Donovan did. The secretary stepped slowly into the room, leaving her hand on the doorknob.

"Excuse me. I'm so sorry, Doctor Montgomery. I'm sorry, Mr. Chandler. Doctor, may I see you in the front office for a moment?" Angel rarely interrupted Donovan when she was with a patient, and she had never asked her to leave a session before.

Donovan, confused by the gentle intrusion, remained pleasant and calm and followed Angel into the front office, which was fortunately empty by then. With her eyes, Angel directed Donovan's attention to the flat-screen television mounted in one corner of the office to keep patients occupied prior to their appointments. The Ghetz trial had concluded, faster than anyone could have predicted or even imagined. The chyron at the bottom of the screen read, "MASON GHETZ WALKS—CLEARED ON ALL COUNTS."

Donovan placed a hand on the back of Angel's empty chair for balance as she watched a swarm of reporters shoving microphones in Jordan Payne's face on his way out of the courthouse. "No comment," he repeated at least three times prior to getting into his car with the aid of a police officer on one side and a chauffeur on the other.

The station's on-location reporter stepped in front of the camera and explained that it was the defense's expert witness, following Donovan's testimony, that had turned the table on the hot-ticket trial.

The reporter said, "As many of you already know, it was only yesterday that the State's professional witness, Donovan Montgomery, blew the roof off of the courthouse here at 26ᵗʰ and Cal with testimony that rocked the country. Montgomery, who is a forensic psychiatrist, law enforcement profiler, and author of a new book that just hit the shelves last week, testified that white nationalist and neo-Nazi Mason Ghetz, on trial for the murders of four young African American men, shot those men because of a bizarre sexual fixation with one of them that included sex for drugs.

"But it was the testimony of the professional witness following Doctor Montgomery that, no doubt, led to the exoneration of Ghetz today. Doctor Sally Jones, noted psychiatrist with degrees from both Harvard and Yale, and who, like Montgomery, has served as a professional witness in several other cases, wowed the jury with the systematic undoing of Montgomery's testimony, claiming that almost none of what the jury heard was true, that there was no corroborating evidence to back her up, and that Mason Ghetz was obviously in fear for his life when he met with those four young men in the Walmart parking lot and shot in self-defense. Mason Ghetz, free tonight, and cleared of all charges."

Angel cautiously stepped behind Donovan, who was still planted behind her chair, staring unblinking at the screen. Angel did not touch Donovan but stood at her shoulder.

Next, the camera cut to Sally Jones as she exited the courthouse, stopping for the camera. This well-respected psychiatrist was stunning and composed, eloquent and polished, the perfect mirror of Donovan in almost every way—except that she was white.

Psychiatrist Sally Jones smiled for the cameras and said, "Today is a good day to be an American."

The crowd outside the courthouse cheered and screamed as if they were at a rally.

"Mason Ghetz is a patriot who found himself in an extremely unfortunate situation," Jones continued, "but one in which he gathered the courage and wherewithal to defend himself. The ugly, black, racist lies that have been hurled at him, intended to taint his name and impugn his motivations that fateful night, are not powerful enough to drown out a community's righteous indignation and the holy truth, which is that there is no place in this grand country of ours for white prejudice."

Again, the crowd erupted, and Sally Jones had to wait for at least sixty seconds before concluding with, "This is a cautionary tale, America. Today, Mason Ghetz walks free, but it might not have come down like this. You know that. You know what kind of madness has seeped into the soil underneath us. Police officers afraid to use their weapons, teachers afraid to teach, young white students denied an opportunity to study at their university of choice because some diversity quota has not been met.

On and on. Make no mistake, today is a good day to be an American, and this is a victory over white racial injustice. Thank you."

As she smiled, waved, and winked, the cameras followed her, but she was done for the moment. Angel slowly picked up the remote control and turned off the television. Donovan was still braced behind Angel's chair, staring at the now black screen. Her secretary and childhood friend knew that this had never happened before. Donovan had *never* been on the losing side of a trial.

Now, the state district attorney's office was marred by the defeat, her reputation had taken a beating, and a seriously disturbed white supremacist with an ax to grind was back out on the streets.

"Jordan's office called. He wants to see you as soon as you can get over there," Angel said softly.

"I don't think that's exactly how he put it," Donovan responded.

Angel leaned her shoulder against Donovan's. "Well, it was something like that. Shall I let them know you're on your way?"

Donovan straightened herself up, finally stepping away from the chair and toward her inner-office door where her patient was waiting. "As soon as Mr. Chandler's session is over," she said.

Angel let out a tiny gasp. "I'm sure Mr. Chandler will understand if you pick up the session later, Donovan. Let me talk to him. I'll just let him know that there has been an emergency and you have to reschedule."

Angel couldn't quite read what was behind her friend's glassy eyes. Donovan stopped outside the office door and turned to address Angel directly. "Thank you for your concern, Angel, but regardless of what else is happening, Mr. Chandler had an appointment with me, and I intend to honor it."

"How can you possibly finish the session?" Angel asked, dumbfounded.

"I compartmentalize," the doctor responded, disappearing into her office and quietly closing the door behind her.

Chapter Nine

The drive from Lincoln Square to the Loop that early evening seemed particularly long. Traffic was dense, and Donovan hit every red light. And as the lauded, brilliant forensic psychiatrist maneuvered her way through the congestion, her mind reeled, trying to make sense of a verdict that betrayed her authority.

Of course, it was not her case to win. As an expert witness, she was merely a cog in a larger machine. Still, when her services were requested, her profiling abilities and medical expertise never failed to convince the jury, regardless of the jury, regardless of the trial. And viewing the situation as if it were a win or lose for the doctor personally, Donovan Montgomery never lost. She *never* lost.

Donovan parked in the LAZ lot on Dearborn. She collected herself and set her mind on the tête-à-tête she was about to have with Jordan Payne. Calmly, methodically, she climbed out of the Prius and took off for the George Dunne Building that housed the state's attorney's offices. As she approached the building, her gaze landed on the Picasso across the street standing sentinel in front of Daley Plaza where a shooting had taken thirty-two lives only days before, a shooting that nearly took her own life.

She entered the building wherein the state's attorney's office was located, along with the seven hundred lawyers who worked for the office assigned to various bureaus. She strolled the long, beige, pictureless corridor, pushed the elevator button, and made her way to her colleague's office. Her demeanor was relaxed, not one muscle tensed, not one hair out of place.

Jordan's secretary glanced up when Donovan approached his desk, a mask of horror and pity washing over his face. "Hello, Doctor Montgomery. I'll let Mr. Payne know you're here," he said sweetly.

Donovan watched Jordan's secretary, Steve Bingham, call through to the inner office. Steve was a young man she had exchanged pleasantries with on numerous occasions over the two years that he had worked at that desk.

After telling Jordan that the doctor was there, he dropped his head a little with the phone pressed to his ear and his eyes on Donovan. "Yes, sir," he said, nodding. Donovan could hear Jordan's agitated voice on the other end, though she couldn't make out whatever venomous words he was spewing at his loyal, polished assistant.

"Yes, sir," Steve said again, mustering a smile for the doctor as she smiled back directly across the desk from him. "Yes, sir," he said a third time and hung up the phone. "Mr. Payne will see you now, Doctor Montgomery." He rose to walk her in, but she spared him the bother. After considering at least fifteen other responses to what she had just observed, she settled on, "I've got this, Steve. Thanks," and continued to the door unescorted.

Once inside Jordan's office, Donovan closed the door but remained there waiting for an invitation before entering any farther.

Jordan was seated at his large cherrywood desk adjacent to the matching writing desk he used as a computer table. Behind him stood the cherrywood hutch with built-in bookshelves atop it. Both shelves were filled with law books and objets d'art he had acquired from his travels through Europe and Asia.

On every occasion that had brought Donovan to this office, she was reintroduced to the over-the-top posh vibe and Hollywood glamour the room emanated. Its architect always injected his personality into his office furnishings. Convinced that not one other attorney of the seven hundred working for the state's attorney had anything grander than a pasteboard desk and ergonomic desk chair that came with assembly instructions and a bag of screws and washers, this room usually made her smile. But not on this occasion.

"Doctor," Jordan said, rising from his desk and walking around its periphery. "Please come in. Have a seat." He gestured to one of the two overstuffed chairs against the far wall, as opposed to either of the two office chairs opposite his desk, while moving to a well-stocked bar cart pushed against another wall of the office. "May I get you a drink?" he asked, pouring himself a scotch and water.

Jordan Payne was controlled in his mannerisms and actions, but his body was as tight as fresh sutures over a deep wound.

"No, thank you," Donovan replied.

She opened her cashmere coat but did not remove it as she sat back in one of the chairs, placing her clutch between her hip and the side of the cushion. Then she crossed her legs, folded her hands on her lap, and waited for the inevitable fireworks display.

Jordan sat in the other chair, crossed his legs, and took a drink from the cocktail glass in his hand. For a moment, they sat staring at one another, both wearing concrete smiles, each shooting icy darts at the other from unblinking eyes.

"Hey," he said, breaking the silence and placing his drink on the small table between the chairs, "let's watch some TV!" And with that, he picked up the remote control, clicking on the television mounted near the ceiling in the corner of the room.

The news was on. Bell Dean was talking to a reporter about the trial and her client's resilience through it all, her impassioned retelling of the case dripping with righteous indignation and hyperbole. They cut to footage of Mason Ghetz leaving the courthouse amid cheering throngs and outraged protesters. His gold tooth caught the sunlight as he smiled from ear to ear for the cameras while guards ushered him through the potentially dangerously crowd in front of 26th and Cal.

Jordan turned the channel. The next station showed a panel of pundits from both sides of the racial divide debating the surprise outcome and how the verdict spoke to the larger societal issues that had been on trial. One side was praising the jury's brave decision. The other side appeared bewildered, with wide eyes and open mouths. One of them said, "What are you talking about? This isn't political. He shot four men dead, three of them in the back of their heads. Tell me one more time what the defense is for that."

Again, Jordan changed the channel. On the next station stood the stunning Sally Jones, professional expert extraordinaire. It was the same clip Donovan had seen in her own office wherein Ms. Jones spoke to the virtues of white America reclaiming its power and the scourge of black racism. She raised her head and clenched her fist as she sermonized this most recent injustice toward a white man defending himself against a gang, outnumbered, and guilty of nothing more than of being white.

One more time, Jordan clicked the remote. Now they were watching tape of Jordan leaving the courthouse. "Oh, this is my favorite show," he said to Donovan. The footage showed Jordan repeating, "No comment" over and over to the pack of reporters stepping over one another to get near him as he struggled to make his way to a waiting town car.

Jordan turned off the television and readdressed his drink. His cell phone vibrated audibly from his suit jacket. He pulled it out of his pocket and turned the device off without checking to see who was calling. "Want to guess how many calls I've gotten over the last two hours?" he asked, neither of them pretending to smile any longer.

Donovan did not take the bait and simply waited for him to answer what was clearly rhetorical.

"I don't know. I don't know how many times," he answered himself. "I took the first two dozen or so, then decided to let the next dozen go to voice mail. I think turning it off is probably the best way to go right now. I think I have a pretty clear idea of what's waiting for me on the other end."

"Jordan …," Donovan finally spoke, hoping to move the discussion forward. But he curtailed her attempt by spitting out another bit of exposition to the scene.

"Do you know how long it took that jury to come back with a verdict?" he asked again rhetorically. "It took them—wait for it—an hour! Yeah, that's right. Closing arguments concluded at about two o'clock, and that jury was out of the chamber and back in the jury box by three thirty. They knew before they got to chattin' what their verdict was going to be, which begs the question …"

Jordan downed the rest of his drink in one long gulp and slammed the glass down on the table. Then he leaned forward and placed his elbows on his knees, stretching his neck out as far as he could toward the doctor poised across from him. "What the fuck?"

Donovan knew she looked somewhat less composed as she crossed her legs in the opposite direction and shook her head. Things were about to get visceral.

"Seriously, what the fuck, Donovan? Everything is hanging on this election coming up. I've got the party chairman breathing down my neck like a frat boy on a third date with the motherfucking prom queen, for Christ's sake. This is a goddamn catastrophe," he said, not quite yelling but no longer speaking conversationally. "This is my ass on the line here. Explain to me what happened."

While he ranted, which Donovan fully expected him to do, she was thinking about the trial and wondering the exact same thing. What had happened? Why had the jury come back before they had even warmed the jury room chairs?

All the doctor could imagine was that some among them had been bought or threatened, told that they or their loved ones would be harmed or killed if they didn't make sure that Ghetz walked. If the ramifications of a guilty verdict were convincing enough, many otherwise good people have been known to make a less than ethical choice in the eleventh hour.

She rolled these thoughts over in her mind while Jordan continued to purge his angst.

"Meanwhile that Make-America-White-Again Diva Defense Attorney Bell Dean and little Miss I'm-gonna-feed-you-shit-and-you're-gonna-ask-for-seconds Sally Jones are the pop stars of the hour. Harvard and Yale, my ass. Maybe those two should be running for office. At the very least they should get a reality show out of this."

Jordan got up to pour himself another drink. "Now with that pile of steaming shit back on the streets, you can bet he's going to become the poster boy for every neo-Nazi organization from coast to coast and around the world. As of tonight, they're all viewing this office as their favorite joke," he said solemnly, "and I'm the punch line."

Donovan ignored Jordan's dramatics and offered what she had been internalizing. "I agree with you that something very wrong happened in that courtroom today, something criminally wrong. Either Ghetz and his brotherhood figured out a way to buy the jury, or he threatened one of them. In any event, we are not dealing with a lone wolf murderer here. There's someone with money behind Ghetz."

With a fresh drink in hand, he returned to the chair and reseated himself, countering with, "Maybe. Or maybe one or both of the gay jurors we so carefully chose turned on us somewhere along the way. I don't know. Look, I thought when you dredged up all that childhood shit that it was going to get us an easy guilty verdict. I believed that information was going to seal the deal."

He was silent and kept his eyes downcast at the glass in front of him. Focused on the ice in his glass, he said, "Damn it, Donovan, I trusted you," his voice breaking with emotion when he spoke those words.

Donovan stopped processing what possibly could have been in those twelve jurors' minds for a moment to address what had become an untenable one-sided conversation. She finally hit her breaking point. So, from where she sat, she decided it was time to share her thoughts with Jordan Payne. She spoke slowly, allowing each syllable to stab the air like an exclamation point.

"You've got some great big balls blaming this on me, you self-centered, self-aggrandizing—*fop*. My God, man, look at you, sitting there slinging insults, puffing out your chest. Honestly, Jordan, listen to yourself. You think you're the only one gonna suffer the consequences of this bullshit decision?"

Jordan reared back in his chair, his eyebrows shooting up a full inch. "Wow. I've never heard you talk like that."

Her expression was flat and cold. "Surprise," she whispered.

Shaking off a response that sent chills down his spine, Jordan tried to salvage the moment from going someplace he had not anticipated, but it was too late.

"Hey, Donovan, listen ..."

"No, you listen. That childhood shit, as you so eloquently put it, is at the very core of the crime and the criminal. It's a pattern of behavior that has been substantiated. He has not yet been tried for the murder of his high school tutor, and maybe he never will be, but I guarantee you he killed him. He's killed other black men, and he is going to kill as many more as he possibly can. Everything I laid out for that jury up through Mason Ghetz's relationship with Peter Darnell is precisely what took place. That relationship was not a what if; it happened. Other people were aware of it. Ghetz's behaviors are well documented. He felt something for Peter—both outcasts, both living similarly dichotomous double lives. He can't deal with those feelings. When he has them, he has to get rid of the source of the emotion; he has to get rid of the evidence, he has to kill. I know what I'm talking about ... Counselor."

Jordan opened and closed his mouth twice without coming up with his next line, so Donovan calmly continued. "One more thing before I leave you to spend some more quality time with your ego. Whatever twist of fate that is allowing Mason Ghetz to sleep in his own bed tonight instead of a cell is the same reason thirty-two people died the other day in Daley Plaza. You can count on it."

Payne took a sip of his drink and gathered his thoughts. "You think so?" he asked softly.

"No," she said, "I know so." Donovan got up and collected her purse. "That's what I do."

Jordan leaped back up. "Hey—hey, Donovan, I'm sorry. I know how good you are at your job. Come on, I know you. Shit, you know me. What are we doing? I know damn well that you've thoroughly considered each nuance and aspect of every testimony you've ever given. Hell, I've watched you stand by your professional opinions even when it meant making a few cumbersome enemies in awkwardly high places." He was referencing Detective DuMont's partner, the cop she helped convict. "This isn't on you, and I know that. This is on me. I just can't figure out what happened at that courthouse," he concluded.

"Something went wrong," she said, moving toward the door. "I will make it right."

"Well, I know you're aware of this, but just to point out the obvious, there is no double jeopardy. No do-overs here. So, I don't see how anybody can make this right. But hey, I will applaud your every effort. Could be we can nail him on related changes. Or we stay on him until he kills again. I agree with you that he will kill again. Maybe we wait for that to take him down."

Jordan followed her to the door. "Hey …," he called out. The doctor stopped and turned. "You really think I'm foppish?"

Donovan rolled her eyes and stepped through the door.

"Listen, let's regroup later tonight, okay? I want to pick your brain on the Ghetz tie-in with the mass shooting."

Donovan was now in the front office next to Steve Bingham's desk, and Jordan was at her shoulder. Steve looked up, immediately absorbed the dynamics, and continued dealing with paperwork as if the two weren't inches from him.

"We'll talk," Jordan said.

"We talked," Donovan said … and kept walking.

Chapter Ten

The wind had picked up, and Donovan felt a serious chill in the air on her walk back to the car. She stopped to give a street person a few dollars and again to bully three teenaged girls into picking up the disposable coffee cup one of them had tossed onto the sidewalk as she passed. All the while, she was calculating, deciding her next move. Mason Ghetz would be sleeping comfortably that night. She knew that he would not be sleeping comfortably for long. Donovan would see to it. But plans needed to be made—important plans. To accomplish that, she needed to find him.

The two easy avenues, work and home, delivered dead ends. Ghetz had been out of work for some time, so there was no place of employment for her to check in with. It had been her experience that most drug dealers kept some kind of job to serve as a cover for their more illegal activities, but this criminal felt no need for such a ruse. And the home address on file turned out to be a vacant lot tucked between two boarded-up houses. She already knew that, having driven by the address prior to the trial.

He had no family. He had no wife or girlfriend. And the person with whom he enjoyed many of his extracurricular activities was lying on a slab at the morgue. Ghetz had put him there.

"Well, you're somewhere, Mason. Game on," she said, window down, radio up.

It took Donovan half the time getting back to her Lincoln Square townhouse as it had getting to Jordan's office in the Loop earlier that evening. This time the lights were with her and the commuter traffic had thinned out dramatically. Driving through the streets of Chicago with "Love On a Real Train" by Tangerine Dream piping through her satellite radio, she felt a good deal lighter, as the weight of the conversation she knew she would be walking into had come and gone exactly as she had anticipated it would. She didn't feel relieved in its aftermath, as she hadn't felt anxious about it to begin with. But she had felt obligated, and now that obligation had been met—paid in full.

She understood Jordan's exasperation at Mason Ghetz being cleared on all charges and the ramifications of that verdict. It meant nothing but bad news for him and his office. She got that. Calling out her professional opinions as suspect—she got that too; she just wasn't about to tolerate it. Even the great Jordan Payne needed to be called out every once in a while.

Now that she had allowed her colleague to vent, she could direct her undivided attention on how to proceed. Donovan never lost a case. This breach of justice had done more than break her winning streak; it had put her professional reputation in jeopardy, tarnished her credibility and the credibility of the state's attorney's office, and put a cold-blooded killer back out on the streets.

Once she was alone with her thoughts driving home, she considered the possibility that this time she might have actually lost a jury that she would have otherwise not lost had she spared them the rather twisted, complicated reason for the killings. She had always reported the facts when being called upon to do so. Was this the one time when *not* reporting *all* of the facts would have served the public interest better?

Ironically, though she had testified many times before, this was an ethical question Donovan had never considered. But the difference between the Ghetz trial and all the other times she had served as a professional witness was that she had never measured what to share and what not to share. Making that distinction hadn't occurred to her this time either. But should it have?

She decided the answer to that was—of course not. That jury could not have been that blown away by the tawdry facts. They'd watched much worse played out on their favorite television shows. They'd been given reports of real-life horrors from their kids on the gruesome, brutal stuff happening at their schools on any given day of the week. No, the jury had not abandoned the doctor's finding as being too fantastic. Nor could those findings have obscured their understanding of the obvious racial component or the ballistics evidence. How could shooting four men in the back of the head ever be construed as a defensive act?

So, Donovan returned to reexamining exactly what had happened. What else was going on that led to that misguided verdict? Who could care about a seemingly insignificant piece of trash like Mason Ghetz enough to pay off a jury? Or maybe he wasn't so insignificant.

Who the hell was Mason Ghetz?

She intended to figure that out, and she intended to step outside of the law to do so. She meant what she said to Jordan Payne; she would, indeed, be making this right.

Entering through the front door of her townhouse, she continued straight into the bedroom, turning on lights along the way. She knew what had to be done. And she could feel herself transitioning into that trance-like mind space she entered when such tasks were necessary. But it wasn't a trance. It was focus—*hyper*-focus.

At her closet, she methodically hung her coat, then undressed, hanging each item, folding her stockings, and returning her shoes to where they were kept in order of color and heel size. Then just as methodically, she opened a dresser drawer and extracted workout clothes. Once they were on, she entered the second bedroom, which also served as her home office and workout room. She was gifted with an engineer's ability to maximize a room's possibilities.

In the corner of the room next to the fold-out couch, a one-hundred-pound Everlast punching bag hanging from an industrial-strength stand waited at the ready. She pulled it into the center of the hardwood floor, strapped on boxing gloves, and made the punching bag beg for mercy as the wheels in her head spun round and round.

Who is Mason Ghetz? Who is he?

When she was sure that the punching bag was down for the count, she ran through some Krav Maga moves to freshen her game. A potentially lethal system of self-defense, Krav Maga had been developed to aggressively finish fights quickly and effectively, not painlessly, as killing your attacker can sometimes be the only way to survive.

Donovan was highly skilled in this self-defense system practiced by law enforcement, the FBI, and SWAT teams alike. In that she worked with law enforcement, finding classes had been easy and accessible when she took up the training years earlier. The combination of her diminutive size and regular dealings with criminals made her an ideal candidate. People of every size and shape could learn these techniques that sharpened reflexes and allowed those who wielded it an almost Herculean advantage over their attacker or attackers.

Though she couldn't get a proper Krav Maga workout without a partner, certain exercises aided in this defense system, and she threw herself into a rigorous round of those. Four skills covered the basics that the defense system was built on and formed the core of the training: 1) Practice your stance: balance is paramount; 2) Practice your punches: rotate hips and shoulders to throw the punch, recoil to a fighting position, repeat; 3) Practice kicks to the groin: lifting the dominant leg, drive the knee forward into the opponent's groin; and 4) Condition the body: cardio exercises of any kind worked.

Her body was conditioned. The punching bag could attest to that.

When first introduced to Krav Maga, Donovan had taken to it right away—the aggressiveness, the lack of negotiation with one's opponent. It suited her. Not everyone knew that she had become quite the devotee that she was, but then Donovan Montgomery remained a mystery to most, and that was precisely the way she wanted it.

There are at least two sides to everything. The same could be said of Donovan. Few people were aware of her many facets. In fact, no one knew them all. Angel, Alfredo, even Jordan had seen glimmers, but none were willing to dip their respective toes in that particular murky pool. Friends and colleagues knew her as the ultimate professional—smart and polished with an almost psychic ability to profile a person or situation with laser-like accuracy. But there were other people who knew the flip side of Donovan.

They were all dead.

On more than one occasion, she had used extreme measures in order to establish justice. Her memory shot back to a time when she had implemented such actions. Wilkie Raymond. He man shouldn't have walked either, not after what he'd done to those girls. But he had. Insufficient evidence, the jury decided.

It had been easy to bait him into a play date that consisted of the same hard-core sexual sadism that had led to the early demise of his young victims. She had allowed him the pleasure of inflicting minor pain on her before she'd flipped the script on him and taken control out of his hands in one heady, exultant moment.

She found a certain poetry in feeding killers the same medicine they fed their victims. This "live by the sword, die by the sword" ideology appealed to her. As did the sense of empowerment she derived from her encounters with such men. God knew her own early life had provided her with a series of painful object lessons in what could happen to the vulnerable, the trusting, the weak. She had been all those things once. She had been just like the young women Wilkie had victimized without being made to pay the price ... or so he thought.

Wilkie Raymond had discovered firsthand that the wages of sin was death. He found it in a motel room with mirrored ceilings and threadbare sheets. She had not rushed it. She had relished it. The only detail she felt badly about was the mess she left for the motel maid.

Donovan dragged the punching bag back to its proper corner and prepared for a long, hot shower. The water beat down on the back of her neck, her hands above her head, fingers fanned, palms pressed tightly against the smooth, red tiles on either side of the showerhead. The smells of lavender and sage filled the steamy room, emanating from the handmade soap she had generously slathered on her skin.

There she stood, thinking, processing, waiting for inspiration. Her eyes remained open and glued to the tile in front of her as an idea began to come into focus. There was a clue in the notes, an unexplored hiding place somewhere among the pages that made up the half-dozen files she had been given on Mason Ghetz before the trial. She was sure of it.

Stepping out of the shower onto a red shag bath mat, she dried herself slowly then applied a favorite lotion before wiping down the shower. She would not usurp any part of her daily routine. That never served her. And when her brain was being pushed to unearth that which wished to remain underground, she became even more methodical than usual.

In her silk dressing gown, she reentered the front room and lit some Nag Champa, allowing the sweet, woody smoke to permeate the air around her. Standing near the table that held her pot stick, she took two deep hits and returned it to the ashtray. Next, in her ritualistic manner, she tuned into the programmed music station that she could count on to never break her concentration with lyrics and banter, only hypnotic techno beats. Now she could begin.

She gathered all of the files and her laptop from the office and arranged everything on the dining room table in front of the bay window brutalized by a brick only days before. Angel had found a window repair service and let them in while Donovan was in court. Now at the table, she systematically went through each file, searching for the missing piece she knew was there.

After wending her way through pages and pages of rap sheets, neo-Nazi affiliations, various meetings and rallies, and other documents that constructed a typical day-in-the-life of the man, Donovan came to what she could only partially access while in the shower. This white supremacist loved to hang out in clubs catering to house music.

She knew something about house music because she knew her city inside and out. House music had been birthed right there in Chicago. And she knew that it had been coined house music because it originated at a club called the Warehouse on South Jefferson near the Loop. This was Chicago trivia 101.

The brainchild of the club's resident DJ, Frankie Knuckles, house music went on to become a popular genre around the world. The electronic dance music had been influenced by seventies funk and soul-styled disco thick with synthesized basslines, electronic drums and effects, and the generous use of sampling.

Donovan knew another piece of history about that club: The Warehouse catered primarily to gay black men. There was a healthy gay Latino clientele as well, but the two-thousand-plus crowds that filled the space on weekends were predominantly gay black men.

The Warehouse had been sold in 1982, and the space became home to another club under different management, but she could imagine that in its heyday, Mason Ghetz had been a steady customer. Obviously, he still held the music in high regard.

She brought herself back to the list of clubs in front of her that Ghetz visited. The list was long, but there were a handful of clubs among them that he spent time at on a regular basis: Smartbar on North Clark, the Underground on West Illinois, the Satin Door on State Street, even the old-school kitsch of Berlin on West Belmont, which was considered dangerously decadent in the eighties and was now catering to neighborhood-friendly drag shows, Queen and Madonna tribute nights, and Pride parties.

And the list of clubs and photocopied receipts she pored over suggested that Ghetz was not intimidated or apologetic in the least about his age and aesthetic, neither of which aligned with the youthful, sparkly regulars that frequented such nightspots. Nothing could be further from the truth. According to the files, he was even considering buying a club before those four dead men became an issue.

There were handwritten notes penned by Ghetz, along with a cache of emails the cops had printed out that spoke to him purchasing one with a man named Bob Lynch. Ghetz had outlined for Lynch what the club could be like. He had even gone so far as to jot down a list of menu ideas.

Authorities had found one unremarkable response from Lynch on Mason's computer saying the club sounded like a cool idea and to give him a call.

Things were getting clearer for Donovan. Her next move had been decided.

Though Ghetz frequented a handful of nightclubs, he seemed to be a staple at the Satin Door. Credit card receipts suggested that this was his favorite hangout. A quick search on her phone informed her that the club was eighteen miles from her front door. She could probably make it there in thirty minutes.

The doctor shut down her computer and stacked the files neatly before returning them to her office. Then she sat at her bedroom vanity and plugged in the curling iron, unfurling her long, thick hair tied up for the shower. While applying makeup, her cell phone rang.

Caller ID told her who it was, Tristan Liaquat. Donovan had met him more than a decade ago while she studied medicine and he studied law. They frequented the same all-night diner and had struck up a relationship that, over the years, had endured every test of time.

As a young girl, Donovan wondered what it would be like to have one of those Harlequinesque relationships—what settling down behind a white picket fence would feel like. Maybe safety, maybe entrapment.

Her youthful experiences with "relationships" had inclined her to think of them as something to be escaped. But when Donovan met Tristan she was no longer a child, and neither one of them wanted anything that required escape.

Though Donovan had once taken a chance on a long-term relationship, she'd learned the hard way that remaining unattached was just simpler, easier, given that the occasional workday required she get blood on her hands. She had no reason to think that Tristan had changed his unattached status either. Answering the call would clarify things.

"Tristan. It's been too long," she cooed into the phone.

"Hey, baby girl. I'm so glad I caught you."

"You caught me years ago."

He chuckled. "You know I want to hear all about the wonderful world of Donovan Montgomery. I see your beautiful face plastered everywhere now that you have that new book out. Congratulations, precious. As it turns out, I'm flying into Midway International in about three hours on a red-eye."

Tris had gone into international intellectual property law. Donovan knew his firm commonly had him make "house calls" for the high-profile clientele they served.

There was a brief silence on both ends of the phone, before Tristan said, "Girl, I know this is short notice. I didn't know about it either until a couple of hours ago. But I'm only gonna be in Chicago for two full days of meetings with a client, then I'm flying back to Atlanta." He hesitated then said, "D, I can't possibly be this close to you and not see you. I *need* to see you."

Donovan had nearly forgotten the effect Tristan's voice had on her. Swimming in his low dulcet purr, lost in the whispered, growling pulse of it, she remained silent.

He took this as hesitation. "Oh, baby, please don't make me beg."

"Tris, you haven't even asked me if I'm seeing anyone."

"Would it matter?"

She considered the tasks in front of her that night. She assessed how long those tasks would take. Donovan concluded that the best way to find Mason Ghetz was to be as focused and clear-headed as possible. Breaking away from this brutal, bloody manhunt for a few hours to revel in Tristan Liaquat's loving company, his sweet kisses and majestic cock was, no doubt, the best way to do that.

"Yes," she finally answered.

"That's my girl! I'll send a car over there to pick you up around midnight, and—"

"No," she cut him off. "I have some errands to run. I'll meet you. Where are you staying?"

"Errands? You know what, I don't care. I'm staying at the Waldorf."

"Of course you are."

"That's right, baby. They're holding one of those cozy little suites for me: fireplace, terrace, private bar, king-sized bed, and a tub big enough for two. I'm going straight from the airport. Get there as soon as you can."

Ending the call, she adjusted herself on the padded bench in front of the black oak vanity. Opening a jar of cocoa butter and her loosely tied robe, she massaged the creamy paste deeply into her calves, her knees, her thighs, and every dangerous curve of her body. She found the elixir intoxicating and knew Tristan did as well, so Donovan made sure to rub it into all the places he would have the privilege of enjoying its smell—and taste.

She stared intently into the attached trifold mirror. After a moment of consideration, she decided that an updo would be a better call and set about pinning and arranging her hair atop her head more strategically this time in a whip of soft curls. She settled on something sexier than a 1960s airline stewardess, but not as sexy as a French film star. Perfect. Securing the ringlets with several bobby pins and a beautiful set of chopsticks, she unplugged the iron and spritzed herself with Tiffany & Co. perfume.

Moving to her walk-in closet, she had only two questions on her mind: What outfit would best transition from nightclub to a sleepover with Tristan—and how was she going to kill Mason Ghetz?

Chapter Eleven

The Satin Door was faceless from the outside with only a small sign attached to the left of the door to identify it. Though a far cry from the more established clubs in which Mason Ghetz spent money, if anonymity were his goal, this club made perfect sense as his go-to. Donovan had no statistics that noted how many patrons had gone missing in recent months. Maybe none had. Maybe he just came here to sell some drugs and make new friends.

Donovan had decided on a three-piece black velvet pantsuit with satin lapels. She wore no blouse under the suit's vest but had opted for a well-orchestrated tangle of three silver and crystal necklaces that draped provocatively over her cleavage. Ankle boots, black leather gloves, and a pink faux fur coat completed the club ensemble. She hadn't been to a club in quite a while, and this journey back in time was one she looked forward to, along with the possibility that she might hit pay dirt and find Mason Ghetz at the first club on her list.

When she arrived, no line awaited her, just a smattering of kids standing in small groups along the front of the club smoking and chatting. Some were black, some white. All of them turned toward Donovan as she approached the door. Some exchanged whispered words. Most recognized her, and for the few who appeared bewildered, their friends explained, quickly followed by affirmative nods all around. *That's right. She was that psychiatrist at the trial*, was the consensus.

Over recent weeks, a few people had started to recognize her because of the TV interview coverage of the new book. Usually, those folks would just smile and wave. Sometimes they would offer a thumbs-up as well. But since the conclusion of the trial earlier that day, she may as well have been on a "most wanted" poster tacked to the corkboard at every post office and Laundromat. One demographic saw her as the woman who made the State lose their case against that Nazi bastard. And on the other side of the coin, she was the woman who said all of those unforgivable statements about that great American, Mason Ghetz.

The videotape of her on the stand and leaving the courthouse the day before was looping endlessly on TV and social media, making her immediately recognizable, especially on that ominous day of the verdict. Her way of dealing with this intimidating judgment was to wear an outrageous pink fur over her velvet suit. "Never let 'em see you sweat" was one of the mottoes she lived by.

"Awesome coat," a young girl called to her when she was close enough to hear. She smiled. The girl and her companions smiled back. And by doing so, that small group of young people let Donovan know that not *everybody* hated her, that shit happens, and that she was truly wearing an awesome coat.

The bouncer barely glanced at her as she pulled her wallet from her clutch to pay him. He had a shaved head, and as he reached into his shirt pocket for a cigarette, she saw a swastika tattooed on the inside of his wrist. A chain dangled from a piercing that went from his eyebrow to his ear, and his white T-shirt seemed too small for his beefy frame.

When Donovan waved money under his nose, he came to attention. Assessing who was standing in front of him, he recoiled, and for a moment seemed to not know how to proceed. He peered over his shoulder into the club as if wanting to hail someone from inside to see the now dubious media darling who had come calling.

Donovan handed him a twenty-dollar bill and said, "My, my. Here you are working, and I thought all you fellas would be out celebrating tonight." She saw the box of wristbands he had next to the money box. "Do I need one of those?" she asked.

He picked up one of the glow-in-the-dark green plastic bands by the end and extended it toward her. "I ain't gonna put it on you," he said. His mouth was twisted and nose wrinkled like he was smelling open sewage.

She gingerly took the band by the other end and walked in, immediately dropping it on the floor as she entered the club.

Once she stepped inside, her identifiability was muted. She trusted the dark room, pulsing lights, and self-absorbed crowd of revelers would make it easy for her to go about her business relatively unobserved.

Marshmello's "Take It Back" blared from a sound system befitting any respectable nightclub, and the lighted checkerboard floor added to the wild-party vibe, different panels flashing on and off in syncopation with the music. As she stepped farther into the crowded room, Donovan could see a smiling DJ working his magic from an elevated perch lit with twinkle lights and neon columns. He danced in place under two mini mirror balls suspended high above him, the shimmering glass orbs spinning slowly to either side of his bobbing head.

Everything seemed typical of any other dance club, but Donovan's radar was picking up signals she couldn't quite read, signals she had started receiving while chatting with the less-than-typical dance club bouncer out front. He didn't fit the rest of the place. He might be right for a different kind of watering hole, but not for *this* place. She stopped for a moment and panned the space again, making a complete 360 from where she stood.

Neon pop art wall sconces, tables tall enough to stand at, couches and upholstered chairs positioned to invite conversation: all of the room's appointments could have been taken directly from the pages of a coffee table book on what a dance club was supposed to look like. Flashy DJ—check, right music—check, kids wearing more jewelry than clothes—check. Her eyes continued scanning, searching for something …

And there it was.

At the end of the bar, hanging on the wall behind the cash register was an 8X10 framed photograph of an American flag. She couldn't recall seeing anything like that in any dance club ever. In American Legion halls, VFW halls, Masonic temples, and any number of other fraternal orders it would seem utterly appropriate. But this was a dance club. Right?

She stared at the flag photo for a moment. It was small enough to be ignored by anyone who wasn't looking for it but visible enough for those seeking the solidarity of other like-minded spirits. *Okay,* she thought, *let's just tuck that in the "What the fuck" file and keep moving.*

As she approached the bar, she took notice of the crowd and staff. The kids on the dance floor were a mix: Asian, Latino, black, and white. But the staff she saw were strictly white. Not necessarily odd in that she hadn't been able to assess the big picture yet. There seemed to be very few servers working the room. But after her meet-and-greet with the employee at the door, she found herself taking note of everyone's ethnicity as if there might be a clue therein. She considered that the bouncer might not have been a white supremacist, but if he wasn't, he should seriously have reconsidered the shaved head and swastika tattoo.

Seating herself at the bar, she noticed two young women toasting one another with what appeared to be pills. They "clinked" the objects, placed them under their tongues, and took sips from the oversized martini glasses each was holding.

The bar was backlit like every other on-trend bar, and to Donovan's discerning eye, management seemed to have stocked a wide selection of high-end liqueurs in addition to all the standard fair. A veritable mob pressed against the sleek black counter, some trying to hail a friend over to join them, some vying for a seat on one of the black satin bar stools. Yet through this chaos, a bartender made a beeline for her as soon as she placed her hands on the smooth granite. Perhaps it was the coat that caught his eye.

Both bartenders and the barback wore black dress shirts and satin ties. Clearly, this was the uniform. But on the bartender who approached Donovan, the ensemble looked particularly incongruous. His shaved head revealed a thick, nasty scar that mapped from at least three inches above his left ear to the middle of his left cheek. The pockmarks punctuating his face were made even more pronounced by the soft light emanating up from under the counter like someone holding a flashlight under their chin for a comically ghoulish effect.

He didn't place a cocktail napkin in front of her, he didn't ask, "What can I get you?" and he didn't smile. In fact, the way he tilted his head back as he surveyed her, she got the distinct impression she might not be all that welcome here. Based on his shaved head and sullen demeanor, the doctor strongly suspected he was in lockstep with the bouncer's sociological and philosophical beliefs.

She studied the bar patrons. No one else fit the profile, only the bouncer and one bartender. Still, she had a hunch, and despite current public opinion, her hunches were seldom wrong. This place was starting to read to her like the stage dressings of a play—a set designed to appear genuine but that was nothing more than a hollow, illusory replica.

In a voice loud enough to be heard over the music and customers, she said, "Hello. I know this is a long shot, but I understand Mason Ghetz comes in here quite a bit, and I happen to be looking for him. Do you know if he's been in this evening?"

He let out an abbreviated guffaw, seemingly surprised by the directness of the question. What was clear by his response was that he knew exactly who she was, and she had been right in deducing exactly who he was—or, at least, *what* he was. Now that both of them knew who they were dealing with, she tried again, confident this time that she was onto something more than she bargained for at the Satin Door. This wasn't only a favorite hangout where Ghetz could score sex and sell drugs, but it employed part of his network. And though it clearly catered to a dance club audience, it had some bigger purpose: a meeting place, safe house, lair, something.

She smiled. "What's so funny? Do you know Mason?"

His mouth and brow curled down.

She tried a third time. "Have you seen him? I'd like to speak to him."

The bartender took out a cell phone and punched a single number. While staring at her, he said to the person on the other end, "Hey, there's somebody at the bar wants to see Mason. She's asking if I've seen him, if he's been in today." He continued staring at Donovan while listening to whomever he was speaking to. "Name?" he asked flatly. She answered, and he repeated the name into the phone.

"That's right … You've got it … Yeah, I thought so too … Yeah, I will … I said I will." With that, he ended the call and slid the phone back in his pocket.

It took him a few seconds longer than it could have to put the phone away and bring his hand back up to the bar, as if he were buying a little time to recalibrate his stance. His eyes were no longer on the doctor. By the time he had one hand reaching for a bar glass and the other reaching for a towel with which to dry it, he had decompressed the muscles in his face while trying on versions of a smile before addressing her again. He then cheerfully said, "You lucked out. Daryl, the owner, will be up here in a minute. Can I get you something?"

His mock civility was chilling. Donovan smiled and declined the cocktail. The bartender then took someone else's order and got busy making drinks but kept an eye on her while she waited.

A Latino kid balanced tentatively on the edge of a barstool next to her had his arms around the waist of a mini-skirted blonde. The blonde had one bright blue patent leather platform on the ground and the other tickling the back of the young man's leg. As she slowly ran her bare thigh up and down his black dress pants, the kid kept his eyes on Donovan, throwing her air kisses and moving his tongue seductively back and forth against his top lip.

Donovan drummed her gloved fingers against the counter deep in thought as she vacantly watched the young cad make a pass at her while simultaneously sliding a hand up the spandex skirt of his *date*. Perhaps she shouldn't have used her real name. She had rolled the dice that Ghetz might be there, or that someone would know where she might find him. But she had not anticipated that the club was a front for something else, that so many of his comrades would be there, and that she might have placed herself in the middle of a minefield. She would have to step ever so carefully.

If the owner had seen Ghetz, would he really be open to sharing that information with the likes of Donovan Montgomery? Was Ghetz actually there, feeling cocky about his vindication and too intrigued to not see her? Donovan's answer to both of those options was no. So, what was this? And what order had been given over the phone that had inspired the bartender's change of heart, unconvincing though it was? At least she had landed where the action was. Mason Ghetz was known here—and so was she.

A man approached the bar through the crowd wearing an open Pendleton over a white T-shirt and holding a can of Pabst Blue Ribbon beer. He did not extend the other to shake Donovan's, but he was smiling broadly. "What a cool surprise," he said. "I couldn't have dreamed you would walk right in here big as life and twice as ugly." Then he laughed. "Hey, that's an old Midwestern expression my dad used to say. I'm not sure what it means. I'm Daryl Hartford. I own this place."

He nodded to the bartender Donovan had spoken to. The man put down what he was doing and dried his hands with a bar towel. "Donovan Montgomery, you are the talk of the town," the owner said, crossing his arms in front of his chest and rocking back on his heels.

"I am?" the doctor asked. "And what is the town saying?" she baited him.

"Well, on the websites I visit, in the chatrooms I chat in, they're saying all sorts of crazy, colorful things. Yes, indeed. Hey, as of a couple hours ago there's even a song about you some dude posted. It's already gone viral. If you hear it, don't pay any attention. He seems like such an angry young man. Ghetz is in the back. We were celebrating. Follow me." He turned and took off.

Was he? Was Ghetz in the back room? Even if he was, the odds of her grabbing a private moment with him were slim to none. She couldn't ask any more questions. She couldn't buy any more time. She could only follow the man or turn on her boot heels and leave.

With Diplo's "Boy Oh Boy" blaring from hidden speakers, she fell in behind Daryl Hartford as the two disappeared into an ocean of gyrating limbs.

He was silent as he led her down a hall past the bathrooms. A line of girls stood against the wall waiting for a chance to pee and privately rework their hairdos in front of a mirror. Then he turned a corner, leading them down another hall, this one narrower and longer than the last. No customers cluttered its periphery. And no doors were evident except for one at the far end of the corridor. As she continued down the hallway, a strong feeling of foreboding washed over her, an instinct that told her she should go no farther.

She stopped dead in her tracks and turned around. The bartender and bouncer moved side by side a few yards behind her, their eyes glued straight ahead, not on her. Neither spoke as they moved in tandem, fists clenching and unclenching every few steps. She turned back toward her host and watched as he disappeared into whatever was behind the one door.

Donovan knew exactly what came next. Her feeling of apprehension evaporated. Her questions regarding what she should or should not have told them dissolved. She nonchalantly pulled at her gloves, making sure they were on securely, then slid her hands into her fluffy pink coat pockets and continued walking toward the door.

The two men caught up to her and briskly brought her the rest of the way, pushing her forward by the elbows. Upon entering, the bartender pushed her hard enough to land her facedown on the concrete floor. The faux fur helped break the fall. She got to her feet as the door closed and locked behind her.

The room Donovan found herself deposited in bore no resemblance to the adjacent club. Two flickering fluorescent tubes illuminated the dank space, which held a desk and chair that appeared to have been exhumed from a trash heap, as well as a hodgepodge of other distressed chairs lining three of the four barren walls. A small plastic patio table stood in one corner holding a coffee can full of sand and cigarette butts.

The concrete beneath her was cracked and stained. Her eyes lit on one large dark red spot in particular. Daryl Hartford noticed her observation. Again, he smiled broadly and said, "Oh, that. Yeah, we had company last week too." All three men shared a laugh over this. Two cockroaches ran across the stain as the laughter subsided.

The bouncer asked the owner, "Hey, Daryl, you mind?" He pointed to Donovan's clutch. "No! Fuck, no. Go ahead, Jim." The bouncer took Donovan's purse and pulled the money out of her wallet. She didn't flinch. He shoved the money into his pants pocket and went back to standing at attention, waiting for his next command.

"So, this is actually a meeting place for you and your pals masquerading as a club?" she asked.

"Are we bonding?" he responded. "We gonna have a chat?"

In that she already knew the answer, she moved to another more pressing question. "Where's Ghetz?" she asked, knowing full well that he wasn't there.

The club owner cocked his head dramatically to one side. "Nigger, Ghetz isn't here. I thought monkeys were supposed to be smart." Again, the three laughed at the doctor's expense. Then Hartford walked behind the desk and extracted a bottle of gin from a drawer. Unscrewing the cap, he stared at Donovan, his eyes glowing with anticipation.

"Man! Doctor Montgomery in the flesh!" he chirped, giddy with his good fortune. "Jim, you got your phone?" He was referring to the bouncer, who nodded affirmatively. "Well, boot that bitch up. I want you to video the fuck out of this."

The bouncer smiled and played with his phone as Hartford drank from the bottle of gin. Then he slapped it down on the desk and stepped around toward Donovan, sitting on the chewed wooden surface.

"Now, nigger, nobody understands where you got that shit you was saying on the stand yesterday, but Mason Ghetz is one badass motherfucker as well as a personal friend of ours, and you tied the rope around your own worthless neck when you threw in your two cents like you did." He shouted to the other two, "Fake news!" to which they responded, "Fake news!"

He chuckled. "Boy, that pretty little Sally Jones ripped you a new asshole, didn't she? She's still at it. I saw her on TV today pointing out every which way that you fucked things up." He paused to make sure Donovan was taking this all in, then offhandedly added, "Now, if you'd gone down on Washington Street like you was supposed to, you wouldn't have had the opportunity to fuck up anything. But you didn't go down."

She had been hoping to come up with another viable answer, but now it was confirmed; she had been the target when all those innocent people were gunned down in Daley Plaza.

"Did you shoot those people, Daryl?" she asked.

"No, that privilege went to a colleague of mine. I wouldn't have missed. And don't call me by my name, nigger." He shook off his disgust and continued. "I'd feel worse about him not killing you if it didn't mean that I personally get to do the honors now. I mean, who doesn't want to be a hero, right? That thing recording, Jim?" The bouncer barked once like a dog. "That's great. Okay, cunt, let's dance."

With that, he jumped off the desk as the bartender stepped behind Donovan, taking a firm hold of her upper arms. The bouncer aimed his camera phone at the floorshow about to take place.

Hartford pulled a knife from his pocket and flicked it open, then stepped close to her face. "I'd ask you if you'd like to say a little prayer before we get started, but there wouldn't be any point to it. Your God ain't in this room," he said, smiling.

The two were practically nose to nose. She smiled back and head-butted him hard enough to send him reeling. As he grabbed his forehead, she rammed her boot into his groin, which brought him to his knees.

Though the bartender held her tightly, the fluffy pink coat was thick. He hadn't thought that through. She pulled her arms out of the coat, leaving him holding it as she whipped around toward him. He flung the garment to the side and doubled his fist, which allowed her all the time she needed to plow into his midsection, throwing him off balance. The dim-witted bouncer tried to hold the camera phone steady while debating if he should abort videotaping and step into the battle or keep recording.

Donovan grabbed the knife that had fallen when the owner collapsed and thrust it deep into the bartender as he tried to regain his footing. He fell, but she knew he wasn't dead. Still, this was her chance to cripple the owner, which she did by pulling the knife out of the bartender and slashing the club owner's face with it. That was easy. She didn't have to go deep at all. When the bouncer finally decided to drop the phone and leap at her, she was ready. He ran right into the five-inch blade.

With her hand still firmly on the handle, she pushed harder and harder, turning the knife as far as she could, inching in as far as it would go from where it was planted deep inside his stomach.

At that point, all three men were on the ground. But she wasn't sure they were dead. She removed the knife from the bouncer, went back over to the bartender, and did what she needed to do to be sure. Then, she wiped the blade on his shirt, folded it away, and slid it back in the owner's pocket. Still clutching his face, he fought to see well enough through the blood streaming down both cheeks to grab her arm, and did.

While he held on to her, she pulled out one of the pretty chopsticks she had in her hair. They were special chopsticks, the ends of which came to sharp points. They had been made especially for her many years ago and had come in handy on more than one occasion. She shoved it in her would-be killer's right eye. She shoved hard. She wanted to be 100% positive that she had driven it through to his brain. She checked his pulse. He had none.

The bouncer, whom she thought she had already killed, continued moaning and writhing on the floor. Donovan knelt next to him on the ground, reached into his pants, and took back her money. "I don't think so," she said sweetly before placing her hands to either side of his shaved head and snapping his neck.

Assessing the room, she first found the phone that had been capturing the moment. Then, she found her clutch. Checking the dead man with the chopstick thrust in his eye, she considered taking a photo of it for posterity but shook her head. "Don't be that gal," she said to herself. Placing the phone in her purse, she snapped it closed.

Next, she retrieved her chopstick and wiped it clean against a small blood-free area of sleeve on Hartford's Pendleton. Without the aid of a mirror, she slid off her gloves, rearranged her hair, and stuck the pretty tool in next to the other one. Sliding her gloves back on, she gave the room one more inspection and decided it was time to go.

Before leaving, she leaned over Daryl Hartford's dead body and said conversationally, "You know—Daryl—it seems a whole lot of folks have been trying to kill me over these past several days. What the fuck made a worthless piece of shit such as yourself think you were gonna kill me tonight?"

Putting on her coat, which remained unscathed by the bloody she-nanigans, she turned off the lights and walked the long corridor to the other hall, which led eventually back into the club proper. Kids were still dancing. It was a little after one in the morning. Everything that had transpired had happened in little over an hour.

The DJ was spinning Calvin Harris's "This Is What You Came For." It was the version featuring Rihanna. As Donovan left through the front door into the crisp Chicago air, she thought how that recording with Rihanna had always been her favorite. She thought about staying a minute longer to enjoy it but there was no time. She had a date.

Chapter Twelve

Donovan located her car and climbed into the back seat. That's where she had stashed the overnight bag and hung the red chiffon blouse on the dry-cleaning hook about the back window. Tristan loved that blouse.

She collected herself. In the shadowed lot, Donovan flipped on the overhead light in the car and assessed any damage that may have befallen her in that back room. The kills had been fairly clean, but she wanted to be sure that not one drop of blood had sullied her hair, jewelry—anything. The coat remained unscathed, having been tossed aside before things took a turn. But the gloves … She removed them, just to be sure, and turned off the light.

In the shadowed lot, she slid off the black velvet vest that had served her well in the club and put on the delicate see-through top. Its buttonholes strained across her firm, bare breasts, and she didn't bother tucking it in. It wouldn't be on long. Getting out of the back seat and into the front, Donovan sped toward the Waldorf Astoria on East Walton Street while Marvin Gaye's "I Want You" wafted from the car speakers.

When it came to suitors—money, status, pedigree, and clout meant little to Donovan. What did mean something was how a man made her feel. Though Tristan was a very straightforward man outside the bedroom, it's what he did to her *in* the bedroom that kept her tethered to him. He was her emotional safe house. Unlike most of the men she knew—professionally, as well as personally—he demanded nothing of her, did not try to manipulate her, and allowed her the bodily autonomy and control that was her life's blood. Their intimacies revolved around what *she* wanted; he seemed happy to provide it, whatever it was, and he never made her feel that she did not deserve to be treated with respect and affection.

Donovan ascended the stairs that led into the foyer of the Waldorf, heading for the concierge desk. Before she reached the counter, a young woman approached, smiling broadly and clutching a hard copy of Donovan's new book.

"Excuse me, Doctor Montgomery. I'm so sorry to bother you, but I just can't believe that I'm looking right at you while I'm holding your book! I'm such a huge fan of yours!"

"Are you now? That's very kind. Are you enjoying it?"

"Am I? Oh, wow, yeah. Yes, I am. Would you mind signing this for me?" the woman asked sheepishly.

"I'd be delighted to," Donovan said graciously, borrowing a pen from the counter.

"Please sign it to Francy. That's what my friends call me. It's short for Frances. Are you here for a convention or a speaking engagement?"

"No," Donovan reported. "I'm … here to see an old friend." Donovan inconspicuously looked down at her watch. "Well, it was nice meeting you, Francy."

In the elevator, Donovan took out her compact and checked again to make sure she had no blood on her face or in her hair. All the way up to Tristan's suite and down the long hall, thoughts of the three dead men back at the club and the elusive Mason Ghetz threatened to rob her of the sexual and emotional escape she craved. But compartmentalizing was one of the things Donovan did best, and she simply wouldn't allow it. Ghetz was not going to take this moment from her. He had taken so much already. *Not tonight, Mason. Not tonight.*

She knocked on the door. Waiting for Tristan to answer, Donovan could already feel the familiar tingling sensation between her thighs that accompanied every thought of the man. When he opened that door, the tingling grew stronger as heat and anticipation washed over her.

Tristan looked exactly as he had when last they met. Six-two with glistening mahogany skin, his muscular, athletic build moved gracefully within the confines of an Armani suit and Prada loafers, the epitome of an African American James Bond. A cocktail comprised of John Coltrane's "Love Supreme" playing in the background, the faint scent of sandalwood, and Tristan Liaquat's million-dollar smile, seduced Donovan before she took a sip of alcohol.

His large hands reached for her, pulled her into the suite, and pressed her against the wall before hellos were exchanged. But she was not ready to be unwrapped just yet. She blocked his fingers just below the bare breasts veiled by the sheer red chiffon of her blouse. Tristan hesitated but did not remove his hands from her slim torso. With her palms over his knuckles, she squirmed playfully.

"Well, hello, Mr. Liaquat. I've missed you too," she purred.

Her subtle movement caused one of the buttons on the blouse to become undone. She glanced down at the exposed valley between the mounds of her breasts, her hard nipples pressing against the flimsy material on either side.

He stared at them as well, spellbound. "Let me in," he whispered as she strained upward against him.

He caressed her nipples with this thumbs, brushing back and forth across them, over and over, as they became more erect. He parted her thighs with one knee. She fought to close them, but she could not. His hot breath was moist on her cheeks as he nuzzled her neck, drinking her in. She trembled. The tingling between her legs became pain—a pain she relished. A low moan escaped her parted lips.

She wanted to make him wait, make him work for it, but her body was taunting her attempt at control. She knew if she let him hold her there one more second, a prisoner of pleasure … "Mr. Liaquat, I am going to come right there against the wall before you even get inside me. I don't think either of us wants that."

He chuckled softly. "You can come as many times as you want, my girl." He lowered his head to nibble her exposed shoulder.

Laughing, she shimmied out of the faux fur coat much as she had at the club, only this time with a smile on her face. Tristan squeezed the soft pile, giving her a look that told her she had won for the moment.

Stepping into the posh suite, she gave it an appreciative assessment. "My, my, Counselor, these are quite the digs."

Flames lapped at the wrought-iron screen of the fireplace, champagne was chilling, and the drapes were parted wide to let in a breathtaking view of the sparkling city below.

"Nothing but the best for you, Doctor. You deserve no less."

He started to step toward her, but she raised her hands to ward him off. "No, no. You stay put. Better yet, why don't you have a seat?"

She grasped the tip of his necktie and guided him to one of the soft leather chairs near the fire. He complied.

"I did not wear all of your favorite lingerie just to have you take me without first admiring it."

She stepped away from the chair, and with Coltrane's accompaniment, she slowly, gracefully stripped down to her thong. Tristan remained silent, occasionally sliding his tongue across his upper lip.

"Now," she said, "let's see how well *you* like being teased into giving it up before you're ready."

His eyes went wide as she straddled him for a lap dance that left him glassy-eyed and sweaty. She gave him access to her breasts then, reveling in the way he caressed, kissed, and nipped at them. She was in control now, feeling the heat, but not letting it devour her. Not yet. Not yet.

When she sensed he was on the verge of coming, she relented, and swung gracefully to her feet. "Tell me, Counselor. Tell me how close you came to losing it."

"Who says I didn't lose it?"

"Aww. You ruined your pretty Armani for me?"

He gave her a look, then rose and went to the bar where he popped the champagne and poured for them both. They retired to the bedroom, bottle and flutes in hand.

He hadn't entirely lost it, for they made love, then made love again. Donovan savored the gentleness of the man, even when she swarmed him, assaulting him with hands and lips and teeth—even when she rode him hard enough to make him gasp. She let him be on top the second time they coupled, relaxed and receptive, knowing she could flip their positions in mere seconds.

She drew the line at letting him pin her arms down, and he knew it. It was a rule of Donovan's road that he had never violated. He might cover her with love bites, but he had never tried to restrain her. She loved that about him. He understood.

Donovan was in no hurry for the night to end. But eventually, it did. Around five o'clock, she started to get out of bed, being as quiet as possible. Tristan put a hand on her hip.

She looked down at him. God, but he was beautiful. "Hey, I thought you were sleeping. I'm sorry if I woke you."

"Where you going, D? It's ..." He groggily tried to look in the direction of the windows. "It's not even light out."

She lay back down, this time on her belly, cuddling up to him so they were nose to nose. "I gotta go. You have a client thing in a few hours, and I've got to get home, take a shower, change out of my party clothes, and take care of some business."

She pushed herself even closer to the man. He slid his arms around her and held her tightly, awake and listening now.

"I've got a lot on my plate right now, T," she said, "and maybe I shouldn't have come over here last night just to steal a few hours, just to be in the same room with you for a while, but I don't regret one second of it. Thank you for a lovely evening."

He levered himself up on one elbow. "Girl, we didn't even get caught up. As de-*lightful* as last night was, you'll have to admit that there was not a great deal of talking going on."

"I know," she agreed, giving him a peck on the forehead and climbing out of bed. "Next time we'll plan this thing out a little better."

"I didn't even get to take you out on the town, buy you a fancy dinner, take you dancing."

She sat on the edge of the bed, looking at him fondly. "Rain check?"

"That's a given, Doctor Montgomery. It's a standing invitation. Hey …"
He grabbed her wrist as she started to rise.

She froze for a second, staring at the large hand wrapped around her
arm. He caught the expression on her face and let go.

"Sorry, D," he said. "I just wanted to say, you look like an Alvin Ailey
dancer. You know that?"

She let go of the prickle of unease and laughed. It felt good. "Wow.
Thanks."

She picked her thong up from the floor and headed for the living room
to collect and don her clothes. Tristan started to get up.

She stopped him. "Don't. Please don't, Tristan. I feel shitty enough as
it is leaving so early—so soon." Falling back onto the bed, she threw her
arms around him, squeezing tightly as she whispered in his ear, "You'll
never know how much I needed you last night. Thank you, T. Thank you."

Donovan left him and maneuvered the streets of Chicago as the sun
peeked out from beneath a dark velvet sky.

"Okay, Doctor Montgomery, time to go to work."

Chapter Thirteen

The following morning, Donovan chose to wear a lightweight harvest-gold trench coat to see Alfredo. It was cold outside, but she wanted to feel that a little bit, let the chill keep her alert and "tight of the punch," as boxers said. She wasn't expecting any punches, but then again, she wasn't *not* expecting any, either.

Making her way to the Prius, she slid on the black gloves she had worn the night before to the Satin Door. She hadn't washed them. Certainly, they were thick with DNA evidence that could attach her to last night's killings. She figured that any traceable evidence would lessen the more the gloves were worn. Besides, she liked seeing them. They provided a visceral touchstone that brought back in technicolor detail each of the three men: their sloppy moves that gave her the physical advantage, their weak efforts to outplay her, and mostly, their bulging eyes and wincing expressions as each of them died at her hand.

It was about nine thirty a.m. Walking across the large taupe-grey slabs of concrete leading to the Cook County medical examiner's office—a large, taupe-grey concrete building—she watched as a man and woman several yards ahead of her entered through the double glass doors hand in hand. She hadn't seen their tears firsthand, but odds were good that one or both of them were or had been crying.

Some people who visited the medical examiner's office did so because they had business with one of the pathologists or other medical professionals who worked there. And people of unique interests visited for a guided tour of the facility. But usually, those who visited the medical examiner's office were about to see the dead body of somebody they knew well.

The people who worked for the medical examiner's office in Cook County were never short of overtime. Chicago had been serving up a perpetual banquet of suspicious deaths since its inception. But the staff remained cordial, even warm, with the people who were called there to identify a loved one.

Donovan entered the building and called out to one of the morgue attendants who was passing through the lobby. "Hi, Mary. You know where he is?" It was a given that she was referring to Alfredo. Everyone knew Donovan. She had spent myriad hours there on a long list of criminal cases and had written up dozens of psychological autopsies for the Cook County Circuit Court as well as private attorneys. And everyone knew that her BFF (were the doctor to have one) was Cook County's chief medical examiner, Alfredo Ramos.

She had no intention of letting him know that she was searching for Ghetz. He would not have supported such a meeting. But a few other questions needed to be addressed, and she knew he would answer them if he could.

"Hey, Donovan. Yeah, I'm going that way. Come with," the assistant offered. The doctor fell in step with the friendly assistant as they made their way toward the suites. "You don't look any worse for wear," the assistant said, nodding approvingly. "That was some beating you took."

Donovan's breath caught in her throat, but she kept walking. She instinctively glanced down at her gloves, then slid her hands in her pockets. "Well, thanks, Mary. What are you referring to?" she asked lightly.

The assistant stopped for a second before continuing down the hall, stunned at the doctor needing clarification. "The trial, of course. Between that attorney and the media, I don't know how you're managing to move around out there at all right now."

Donovan grinned, breathing in deeply. "I believe that everything will sort itself out in time, luv. One day at a time, right? That's all you can do."

Mary and she parted ways with abbreviated waves and smiles when they arrived at the autopsy suite where Doctor Ramos was working.

Few people would be able to saunter into the medical examiner's office and head anywhere they chose, but Donovan Montgomery was the exception. Even city officials were not allowed to walk into an autopsy suite during an examination, but Donovan could, and did, whenever she had serious business to discuss with Alfredo—or wanted to change dinner plans—or was unsure as to which Louboutins she should invest in next.

Donovan entered and closed the door behind her but remained where she stood, careful to not sully the procedure that was taking place in the middle of the room. "Morning, Alfie," she said, smiling at her industrious friend. Alfredo was holding a vibrating electric Stryker saw in both hands directly over the head of the dead man splayed open atop an aluminum table.

He glanced up, making eye contact with his guest, then with a professional's polish, cut off the top of the man's head. He had already run a scalpel from behind one ear, across the fellow's forehead, and around to the other ear, having pulled the flesh from the skull in two tidy flaps: one resting over the corpse's face, the other dangling over the back of his neck, which was propped up on a body block designed for such procedures.

"These vibrating saws are brilliant. They allow you to slice right through the skull without disturbing the cerebrum," he said softly.

The dead man's chest cavity was exposed and emptied of all its organs, which were in a large aluminum tray on a table next to the body.

"I think the gentleman has other issues right now, Doctor," Donovan quipped.

Alfredo smiled but did not pull himself away from the matter at hand. "You have found me at a rather precarious juncture, my princess. Forgive me for not giving you my undivided attention, but duty calls. That said, what can I do for you, Doctor Montgomery?" He placed the saw on a tray that held other tools of the trade and picked up a butter knife with which he gently pried off the skull cap, exposing the brain.

"Did you hear about Ghetz?" she asked.

Once the round piece of skull was lifted from the head, the chief medical examiner exchanged the butter knife for a scalpel and began working through the soft membrane that was still attached to the bottom of the skull cap he had just created.

"Yes," he answered with a twinge of disgust in his voice. "Yes, I heard. I called you. You didn't answer. You okay?" he asked as he carefully began to sever the sheath connecting and covering the cerebellum and occipital lobes to the spinal cord.

"Yes," she said, but he could hear a trace of a "but" in her one-word response and peered up at her, momentarily veering his attention from the thin membrane he was gradually freeing from the top of the dead man's spine. "Tell me," he said, turning back to the body and scalpel.

"Ghetz likes to hang out in dance clubs."

"That guy? Dance clubs?" Alfredo asked rhetorically.

Donovan continued. "I got lucky and found one he frequents. I was able to chat with some people who know him, people who know a whole lot about a whole lot of nasty things. And I now have it on high authority that … that *I* was the target of the shooting in Daley Plaza."

He finished with the scalpel, placed it on a tray, and easily lifted the dead man's brain from what remained of his head. Holding the brain in one hand, he regarded her sternly. "You have to tell the cops," he said. "If you don't and you're right about this, that's a clear obstruction of justice, Donovan."

They stood facing one another from across the room. Donovan averted her gaze to the floor, but Alfredo kept his on her. Then he extended the brain in his hand toward her. "Here, take this, I'm going to call them myself."

She shot him a mock mask of shock, raising her hands and shaking her head.

He withdrew the brain. "Seriously, you have to call them, darling. You could get in a great deal of trouble. You don't need any more of that right now."

She took a small step farther into the room. "I don't want the cops, Alfie," she whispered. "This is personal. And besides … look, I don't have anything *solid*. The cops couldn't put anyone away yet." She could see her words were not changing her pal's mind at all. "But, hey, things are getting clearer, right?"

He placed the brain in a shiny shallow aluminum bowl and turned back to her. "So, thirty-two people died in an effort to keep you from testifying. That it?"

She nodded. "I suppose the rationale was that with a mass shooting, nobody would know there was a specific target. The event would go down as another random act of violence. But the crazy motherfuckers didn't kill me. They killed thirty-two innocent people."

Alfredo shook his head. "Hard to believe that was only a week ago."

Donovan's typically unfurrowed brow pinched slightly. "A week and a day. Have you been able to confirm where the shots came from?"

Taking off the surgical gloves he was wearing, Alfredo stepped to a closed metal trash can, opened it with the pedal at the bottom, and threw them out. "Yes. Temple office building, just as you figured. Came from the twenty-first floor." He moved to the sink and washed his hands. "It's not in the news yet, but it will be by the afternoon, I assume."

Pulling two paper towels from the paper towel dispenser, Alfredo turned to face Donovan while leaning against the counter and drying his hands. "They found two bodies in the closet of one of the offices: a cleaning lady named Hannah Bird, and Saul Jacobson, the guy whose office it was. They're pretty sure it was one shooter. The killer shot Hannah and Saul before setting up shop, cut out a pane of glass in the window just big enough to accommodate the automatic, then sat there overnight—waiting."

"A cleaning lady and a businessman," Donovan reiterated.

"Hannah and Saul," Alfredo clarified. "I met Hannah yesterday. Today, I'm spending some time with Saul." He indicated the aluminum table holding the dead man whose organs were in a large metal tray and whose brain was sitting in a bowl a few feet away.

Donovan could see the man from where she stood near the door.

She took two steps toward Alfredo and stopped. Alfredo knew that whatever had brought her there that morning was now going to be discussed, and stepped toward her as well. They were now inches from one another, face-to-face.

"Do they know who the shooter was?"

"I don't think so. If they do, I haven't heard it."

"Weapons?"

"Hannah and Saul were shot with a Glock. An AR-15 was used in Daley Plaza. It's the gun du jour. A few years ago it would've been a MAC10."

"A MAC10 doesn't have the range the gunman needed."

"Correct."

"So now that we know I was the target ..."

"You think there's a connection between Ghetz and the mass shooting."

"Well, he's swimming in the same swamp. If all those people were killed to keep me from testifying, there's got to be somebody over Ghetz, somebody who was willing to put up a buttload of capital to get that piece of shit back on the streets. Who could possibly care?"

Alfredo considered that for a long moment. She watched the wheels turning in his head, hoping he'd have some insight, that he'd be able to uncover some small *something* that she hadn't yet unearthed.

"Donovan, in all of those notes you read on Ghetz, was there a name? One name anomalous to all the others?"

"In what way?" she asked, already riffling through the files in her head, searching for an answer to a question she wasn't clear on.

"Maybe ... maybe a name that seemed anomalous in context with all of the drug-dealing Aryan brothers he commonly associates with."

Donovan remembered the email about the aborted club idea. "There was one, a guy named Bob Lynch. But he didn't end up working with Ghetz.

Ghetz asked him to put up some money for a club, and the man said he would talk to him about it but never did."

"Why did he choose to hit up Lynch for the money?" Alfredo glanced at Saul Jacobson then at the clock on the wall. "Well, there could be a dozen reasons, I suppose," he said, dismissing his own question.

As he pulled another pair of surgical gloves from a box next to the sink, he asked, "Who paid for Bell Dean? Not the public defender's office."

"I don't know," Donovan answered. "You think whoever paid for his defense team is behind this whole affair?"

"Don't you?" Alfredo glanced at her from the tail of his eye. "Of course you do."

She shrugged as she watched him work one glove and then the other securely around each finger. "Okay, seems obvious to me, but I'm checking my assumptions. So, what if it was Lynch? Why would he go to all that expense?"

Alfredo had picked up some instrument from the tray next to the brain and began probing it. "I don't know. Maybe Mason Ghetz doesn't only fancy young black men. Maybe his proclivities include club owners. Maybe Bob Lynch has a vested interest. Whatever it is, you might want to take a closer look at that relationship."

Slowly nodding her head, Donovan turned to leave. Before she reached the door, there was a knock, and Mary appeared on the other side. She stuck her head in the room and said, "Sorry to interrupt, Doctor, but I just wanted to let you know that three bodies were just delivered."

"Of course there were," he said sarcastically. "We may be the only three people left standing in Chicago. What do we know, Mary? Anything?"

Smiling, Mary shared what she knew. "Not *really*. The bodies were discovered this morning by—a delivery guy? I'm not sure. Bernice knows more. She's working on the paperwork now. You want me to have her fill you in?"

Alfredo continued to probe the brain. "No. I'll wait and be surprised. I have to start recording my notes on this. Donovan, would you push that foot pedal over a few inches toward the action here?"

Donovan was quick to comply. She pushed the pedal over with her foot until Alfredo could reach it.

"Okay. I'll be up front," Mary said, starting to close the door. "Oh, the Satin Door! That's it," she blurted out.

"What does that mean?" Doctor Ramos asked.

"Where the bodies were found. A dance club called the Satin Door. Nice to see you, Doctor Montgomery." The morgue assistant smiled at Donovan and closed the door.

Alfredo stopped what he was doing, frozen in place. Donovan froze as well. After a tense moment of silence, she stepped closer to her friend, who did not look up at her. He kept his eyes fixed on the tool in his hand. She took one more step nearer and waited, calculating his next move—and hers.

Would she have to use Tristan as an alibi? She hated to do that—hated to drag him into this, perhaps ask him to lie about when she came to his suite, but …

Alfredo placed the metal stick he had been using on a tray and fumbled with the other instruments, touching one then the other without picking anything up. Then he froze again, placing both gloved hands to either side of the bowl that held Mr. Jacobson's brain.

Donovan held her breath.

With a grimace on his face, he slowly exhaled and stepped on the foot pedal that operated the recorder he used to dictate his autopsy notes, and began doing so.

Donovan could feel her muscles relax. She reached out and squeezed his arm, planting a light kiss on the shoulder of his lab coat before leaving.

Retracing her steps down the hall toward the front doors of the building, she now knew that somebody had been aiming at her from the twenty-first floor of the Temple Building across from Daley Plaza. But she didn't die, so the killer, or whomever had hired the killer, had quickly secured a camera-friendly defense counsel (and maybe a jury member or two) to discredit her testimony, shut down the embarrassing, unnecessary truths she was broadcasting about him, and kept Ghetz a free man. If anybody wanted her dead now, it would be out of spite rather than to shut her up. After her antics the night before, probably even more skinheads and the like were waiting in line for the pleasure.

Sorting through Alfredo's thoughts and her own, she now understood the board she was playing on. She just needed to find the missing pieces, i.e., who had paid for Ghetz's counsel and who wanted him free. Locating Mason Ghetz was the game, the stakes were dangerously high, and figuring out if Bob Lynch was a person of interest was the next move.

As she stepped back out onto the large slabs in front of the Cook County Medical Examiner's Building, she saw Detective James DuMont approaching. Her razor-sharp focus would have to be momentarily redirected away from the whereabouts of Bob Lynch and aimed at the detective. Dealing with Detective DuMont always required her full attention.

"Doctor Montgomery, why am I not surprised to see you here?" he asked in lieu of a more conventional hello. "This is very convenient. I was going to be calling you in a little while. Providence," he proclaimed. "Yeah, it must be providence running into you like this. Do you have a minute to talk?"

Their trench coats met up as the two stopped directly in front of one another, hers punctuating the barren walkway, his blending in seamlessly with the concrete beneath him.

"What can I do for you, Detective?" she asked dryly.

"Three bodies were just removed from a dance club over on State Street called the Satin Door. Looks like all three were involved in this white-supremacist business that seems to be monopolizing the department's time lately. One of them was apparently the owner, a guy named Daryl Hartford. You know him?"

"I'm a black woman, Detective. I can honestly say that I don't fraternize with one single white supremacist."

"Have you *heard* of him?" he countered, without adding "smartass," which he conveyed with his expression.

"I don't recognize the name. Should I?"

"I understand you were at that club last night, Doctor."

Donovan could've stumbled around with a "why do you think that?" or "no, I wasn't," but she knew that all he had to do was flash a photo of her to the other bartender or any number of other people there the night before. She was easy to pick out of a crowd. If she'd cared about not being recognized, she would have made an effort toward that end. At the very least, she would have left the pink faux fur at home.

"That's right, I was," she affirmed.

Detective DuMont adjusted his hat, pushing it back farther from his forehead. "You mind telling me what brought you to that club, Doctor?"

She broke her stare, casting her eyes toward the street for inspiration, then back to the man in front of her. "I just love house music."

A vacuum of silence sucked at the cold air between them.

"You have a problem with my taste in music, Detective?" she asked, waiting to see how far he was going to take this, and wondering how far she would have to go to cover her tracks.

He smiled. "No," he said. "I don't have a problem with your taste in music. I do have three dead skinheads and no suspects. That's a problem."

She nodded in agreement. "Yes, that is tricky."

"So, you sure you didn't see anything suspicious while you were there? Dancing to the house music?"

Donovan wished him well with the investigation and began walking toward her car.

"I thought you might have seen something, heard something. That's all," the detective tossed out lightly as she passed him.

Before she got too far from where they had been conversing, he called out to her. "Doctor ..."

She stopped.

"One of those guys had his neck broken. Another one had his skull bashed in against the concrete floor, and the third, same thing, only—he had an eye put out with something long and pointy, maybe something like the heel of a lady's shoe. I don't know. Can you think of something that might do that kind of damage?"

They were now, once again, locked in each other's gaze, this time from about twenty feet apart.

"It could have been any number of things. You know that," she finally answered, adding, "What a nasty mess you've been left with. I am sorry."

Still smiling, he asked, "Sorry about the mess, or ..."

DuMont was running out of ways to bait her into coming clean. He knew how she operated. He knew she was Teflon. To him, the murders at the Satin Door absolutely smacked of Donovan Montgomery's handiwork. But, as usual, when it came to her handiwork, he had nothing to hold her on. She knew that. She understood James DuMont as well as he understood her, so she turned and kept walking.

"Okay, then," he tossed out, watching her leave. "You let me know if you think of anything." She waved without facing him or slowing down.

"Feels like a vigilante to me," she heard him say.

Chapter Fourteen

Climbing into the front seat of her Prius, Donovan finally took a deep breath. She felt as though she had been maneuvering through a minefield since arriving at the Cook County medical examiner's office that morning. Though she had gotten what she came for from Alfredo, and had successfully dodged Detective DuMont's (informed) insinuations, the interactions had been more complicated than she would have liked.

Nevertheless, she had made it out unscathed. And now she was safe—and alone—inside the sanctuary of her clean, comfortable car. Not only would the vehicle get her away from there, but driving often provided her time for some especially transcendent introspection. Depending on how long she sat behind the wheel, she could commonly plumb her subconscious for advice and direction. Right then, she needed both.

But as she pulled out onto West Harrison toward South Oakley Road headed for her office, her thoughts did not rush back to Bob Lynch, Mason Ghetz, or any of the other high-voltage activities of the past several days. Instead, she was struck by a wave of regret, an emotion Donovan Montgomery rarely entertained.

She hadn't always been so aloof, so machine-like. She used to have easy, unguarded conversations. Often she met with people, people she considered friends, without having any agenda at all. In fact, there was a time when she had regularly called Detective James DuMont "Jim" and went shopping with his now ex-wife Monica. There was such a time.

She had always dealt with a rather pronounced obsessive-compulsive nature; her affinity for ritual and patterns was part and parcel of the OCD and with her darker compulsions. Yet another part of her—a part that laughed and cried easily, enjoyed walking barefoot in the sand framing Montrose Harbor, and got a big kick out of displaying an ever-expanding collection of exotic, colorful bongs—was nowhere to be found.

She could barely access the memory of that other self, but once in a while, when she least expected it—like right then on the heels of seeing her old friend James DuMont up close and eye to eye—she remembered. When exactly she had changed was less clear. But she knew for certain that the last straw was laid no further back than six years. That's when the relationship she was in had started to go bad—very bad. A year later, he was dead. And when he died, so did that part of her that had the capacity to be carefree.

Tom Karp was a young detective and third-year veteran with the Chicago Police Department when he and Donovan met. She was working on one of her first high-profile cases involving a serial killer whose targets were predominantly on the west side, and Tom was busy working on the same case.

A warm, funny guy with soulful eyes and a broad smile, Donovan liked him right away. But Tom fell in love. Tom fell hard.

Donovan recognized that, and a few other facts, about this man straight-away: He was relentless in his pursuits (her heart being among them), he believed that he harnessed great skills of manipulation (that she always saw through), and he needed her. Joining the force did not afford him the sense of self-worth that he anticipated. But he found his purpose with her at his side.

Tom Karp was devoted, faithful, charming, and shared a professional landscape with Donovan, which meant they understood each other's language. On paper, a long list of attributes and commonalities made Tom her perfect partner. The fact that she didn't love him was dwarfed by that impressive list. As months passed, he was able to negotiate her affection into a relationship.

When they decided to move in together, Donovan wanted to live in Bronzeville. Tom, too, considered Bronzeville a great place for them to start a life together, and it was comfortably close to the police headquarters over on South Michigan. Then, Tom found a nice apartment on 37th and Indiana, which, he later pointed out, was even closer to police headquarters. He rented the place without telling her because he wanted to surprise her.

She was surprised—surprised to discover that he had chosen a neighborhood other than the one they had decided on together, and had rented an apartment without consulting her. She was surprised it had taken this for her to recognize the serious control issues that had been on display even before they shared a roof. She was surprised at the depth of his possessiveness, which she knew to be a black hole of insecurity. Above all else, she was surprised that—knowing those things—she packed her bags, turned in her keys to her landlord, and made a home with the young detective.

Over time, what began for Donovan as nothing more than a maternal affection, morphed into love—depending on one's definition of the word. Her constant efforts to bolster his pride and growing desire to protect him, mainly from himself, only seemed to amplify his possessiveness.

Emotional cruelty had entered the arsenal that he aimed at her daily. Alarm bells were going off in her heart, head, and soul, but she ignored them, whistled over them, and silenced them.

Donovan's first best seller on profiling and two convictions based on her expert testimony came one after the other, within a year. The fact that Tom's career was at a standstill while he watched her become a superstar in the field of forensic psychiatry only fueled the tensions between them.

Still she stayed. She forgave him. She loved him through each tongue-lashing he gave her, certain they only scarred his psyche, not hers. She sublimated her emotional responses, falling back on the skills that had enabled her to survive an abused childhood, skills she had brought with her into adulthood because they worked, they were tidy, and they kept her sane. She compartmentalized, and so, though the power dynamics of the relationship grew more and more volatile, the sex remained spectacular, and the love abided.

One particular evening, Donovan arrived home to a recorded loop of ocean sounds coming from their stereo system and filling the apartment: gentle surf, crashing waves. The volume was set higher than one would normally play something like this, and she stopped for a moment to take it in. She decided she rather liked it. She had never heard it before, but the sounds of the ocean had always been soothing to her, and she found the nature music immediately calming.

Clearly, Tom had planned this for her. Just then, she received a text from him. "Let's play," was all it said. Grinning, she placed her purse, coat, and briefcase on a club chair as she slowly approached the bedroom and gently pushed open the door. White candles cast the only light. Nag Champa filled the room, a thin strand of woody smoke snaking from an incense burner near the door. The bed was covered in fat, white feather boas, and Tom was propped up among them, naked and smiling, holding a glass of champagne in one hand and a pair of handcuffs in the other.

"I'd love to see *you* in these tonight," he said coyly.

Her smile froze on her face. "No."

"Why not?" he asked, his voice wheedling. "I'll play nice."

Play. Others had used that word to describe what they did to her. "You know why."

He shrugged, setting the cuffs on the bedside table. "Never hurts to try."

Never hurts? She shook herself. *Let it go. You love the guy, let it go.*

Wordlessly, Donovan slipped out of her business suit, leaving on her filmy bra and panties to allow the gentleman the pleasure of removing them. She crawled through the soft feathers toward her lover's parted lips. His chest rising and falling with each deep breath, he watched her come nearer, sliding her hand along his bare skin.

The phone rang.

It wasn't Tom's primary cell; it was the other one, the one he kept in the bedside table. Much to Donovan's amazement, he handed her the champagne flute and scrambled to answer it.

"Yeah," he said into the cell. He stood naked at the bedside, head down, his other hand on his hip. Donovan was under the impression that this phone was for work emergencies, and in that he was more than willing to forfeit a night of passion to take the call, she braced herself for the worst.

"He said what? No. No, I'm going to take care of this shit. I told him I would, and I meant it." Tom ended the call and turned to his lover, trying to smile. "Honey … Sweetheart, I'm sorry, but I'm going to have to go. I don't know when I'll be back."

Sitting cross-legged in the bed of feathers, she smiled and nodded, hiding her concern. "What's the problem?"

He leaned over and kissed her on the forehead. "You know I can't talk about it," was his answer. He threw on his clothes and coat, grabbed the phone and his gun, and left.

As she sat pondering the situation in his absence, a few unsettling thoughts ran through her mind, but she allowed them all to evaporate. She removed the boas, slipped under the covers, and went to sleep. At least they weren't fighting.

Shortly after that, Tom bought two new cars, one for each of them. Over the next few months, he showered Donovan with designer clothes, jewelry, and nights on the town, indulgences that couldn't be had on a cop's salary—indulgences he refused to allow her to supply from her ample income. The more gifts he bought, the kinder Tom became. His abusiveness and hypercontrol seemed to ebb in proportion to the mysterious influx of money. Donovan was happy that they were getting along better than they had in a long time, but she knew something was wrong. If he was not controlling her, then where was that compulsion spending itself?

For a while, she chose to turn a blind eye toward the situation, to play dumb. But she was a psychologist—a seasoned profiler, for God's sake. It didn't take long for her own culpability to prod her into action. So, she took matters into her own hands. Not just because of some ethical or moral imperative, but because she had a professional reputation to protect. If something illegal was going on under her nose, it did violence to her credibility as a profiler.

Her first move was naive. She simply called Tom out. He denied any wrongdoing and claimed he had been gambling and didn't want to tell her, adding that he was obviously lucky, so she shouldn't complain. But after she questioned him, his behavior became more erratic, more abusive, and they were back to where they had started before his "good fortune."

Her next move was to tail him. That turned out to be easier than it should have been. To his credit, Tom was not a very polished criminal. His "emergencies" were taking him to Riverdale. She watched him go into a convenience store and come out, sticking an envelope in the inside pocket of his leather jacket. A few doors down, he entered another mom-and-pop store and came out with another envelope. She couldn't bring herself to believe he was doing what he appeared to be doing.

She then followed him to an apartment building over on Tracy Avenue. There, he parked in front of the building and waited. A young black kid came out of one of the apartments and approached Tom's car. The kid appeared to be maybe twelve years old, Donovan assessed, maybe thirteen. Some sort of verbal exchange took place, and the kid sauntered sheepishly back to the apartment building.

Donovan didn't need to witness any more of these stops. She decided, however, that other information was necessary before proceeding much further.

The Office of Professional Standards was an agency that investigated complaints about cops. Most civilians didn't know about OPS, and those who did commonly thought it existed only to clear dirty cops and those accused of police brutality. Donovan leaned toward agreeing with the latter sentiment. She had never been inspired to know much more about it until then.

Indeed, a complaint had been filed against Tom. Donovan wrote down the woman's name and address and paid her a visit the following day.

According to the woman, her eighteen-year-old son was in jail for drug possession that she and the young man claimed had been planted on him by Tom Karp. The youth had no prior convictions. This happened, the woman explained, because she had been unable to pay the detective a thousand dollars in "protection money."

There it was. Detective Karp was systematically extorting money and favors. If they didn't pay, he would plant and discover drugs on people whom the system found highly suspect anyway (meaning black, poor, and desperate), and no one would think twice about disbelieving what the accused had to say in their defense. The neighborhood had quickly learned to fear Detective Karp, as he had put several young men away over a short period of time.

Donovan deduced that Tom could gain access to the warehouse shelves of the property room where confiscated drugs were stored after trial and slated for incineration. It was likely that was how he had gotten hold of the drugs, but she wasn't sure.

Detective James DuMont was sure. He was Tom's partner.

When he called Donovan and asked her to meet him, she knew by his voice that something was troubling him. She was right. Not only was his young partner swimming in a cesspool of his own making, and further crippling an already limping community, but his partner's girlfriend was about to turn him in. He begged Donovan not to do that, as he believed he could get Tom to turn his life around and keep him from losing his badge.

Donovan thought about the ramifications. Then she thought about Tom's bullying tactics and wondered how many young lives he had forever scarred, how many families he had torn apart—black kids—black families. How could he do that to his own people?

She turned him in. She wore a wire. Her testimony, along with that of the woman who had filed a complaint, sealed his fate. Tom was convicted and incarcerated. A week later, he was dead. It was logged as suicide. Donovan did not believe that to be the case.

Neither did Detective DuMont. And he never forgave her.

She remembered all these details on her drive back to the office. And as she turned onto West Lawrence Avenue, then right onto North Lincoln, she realized that tears were running down her cheeks. She hadn't cried in years.

She collected herself while parked in front of her office building. It was nearly two p.m. on a Wednesday. The workweek lunch crowd had retired back to their desks by then, leaving the street pleasantly empty. Cataloging the dark cloud that she had just driven through, Donovan flipped down the visor above the steering wheel and reapplied her lipstick, dabbed away the mascara from under her eyes, and ran a hand through her hair. She had a lead; it was a long shot but worth a small gamble. She would soon be paying Bob Lynch a visit on the outside chance that he could lead her to Mason Ghetz.

Angel glanced up from her paperwork as Donovan entered the waiting room. Her eyes got big and brows raised as she started to say something that she was not afforded enough time to say. Donovan cocked her head a little, seeing the signal, but the answer became evident before the doctor got more than two steps past the door.

A reporter leaped up from one of the waiting room chairs and extended a hand to shake Donovan's. Angel tapped a pen on the desk, defeated. The reporter towered over Donovan, standing well over six feet tall, and was quite thin. He appeared to be in his midthirties with a pleasant but urgent look about him.

"Donovan Montgomery, hi, I'm Eugene Hoffmeyer from the *Chicago Sun-Times*. I was hoping to have a word with you about the trial."

Angel gave Donovan a small shrug and readdressed the work in front of her. Donovan shook the man's hand tenuously, taking in his dated shag haircut and fat polyester hipster lapels, thinking that they somehow looked appropriate on him. "That's been fairly well covered, Mr. Hoffmeyer. I don't have anything to say."

"Well, you've offered your insights on twenty-five other high-profile cases, and every one of those trials ended with a guilty verdict. That's an impressive record, Doctor."

"Hopefully, justice was served," she said.

"You're always on the winning team, Doctor Montgomery. What happened in there? Who was that jury? Right? I mean, that's the question, isn't it? White supremacist shoots four black kids in the back of their heads and walks." He snorted a brief chuckle. "WTF, right, Doctor? And where in the world is Mason Ghetz? He won. He's in the clear. I thought it would really be something to speak with him directly. Get his thoughts on the verdict, but—man—he's *gone*. Why do you suppose he went underground? It's all just a hell of a mystery, if you ask me."

"Mr. Hoffmeyer, I don't mean to be rude, but I am a little busy today …" He glanced around the empty office. She kept her eyes on him. "And I really don't have anything for the *Sun-Times* that I didn't already say when the trial concluded. Now, if you'll excuse me." She started to move away, but he blocked her.

"See, I was thinking that you might after what happened today."

He had her attention.

"Who made up that jury?" Once he was sure that she was listening, he relaxed and stepped back. "I thought that might make a good story. I'm thinking that just the fact sheet on the guy should have inspired a longer deliberation before twelve people became unanimously convinced of his innocence. And that's not even considering the compelling facts you were brave enough to bring to the table. Brava, Doctor, really, that was effing amazing stuff."

She began to speak, then chose against it and started once more to move away. Again he blocked her.

"So, what were those folks thinking? I thought I'd find out. Maryanne Briggs was the first juror I looked up. Unfortunately, she died three days ago. Seems she had a heart attack, poor old gal. Well, she was in her sixties, had a history of heart trouble. Of course, my dad and mom are in their sixties and they're both fit as fiddles. Never know, right? And Maryanne didn't even have a chance to use some of that money of hers to try and get any fancy medical care, she went that fast."

Angel put down her pen, all at once attentive to what this reporter had to say. Much to her chagrin, Donovan, too, found herself invested in Eugene Hoffmeyer's information. "Go on," the doctor said begrudgingly.

"Yeah, according to her sister, she came into some money a couple of weeks ago, a little pocket of money, cash, a few grand, but for a gal on a fixed income, that could've helped. Her sis asked her about it, but Maryanne got a bit—*shy* about answering. That's the way I heard it."

Donovan decided that she rather liked this abrasive, smart, dedicated journalist, but she had no intention of letting him know that. Soberly, she said, "And you're about to tell me that no one can trace where the money came from, is that right, Mr. Hoffmeyer?"

A huge smile spread across his face. "That's it, exactly. Curious, isn't it?"

She wouldn't give him the nod he was waiting for, but she didn't run, either. "And what happened today, Mr. Hoffmeyer?"

"You know, it's just a crazy coincidence, I suppose. I contacted a couple of the other jurors, just going down the list of twelve names, and when I tried to contact number five, Dirk Cameron, I was told—wait for it—that he died last night. Car accident. Hit and run." He stepped closer to Donovan and leaned in. "Isn't that wild?"

Donovan and Eugene held each other's gaze for a moment, then she straightened herself while unbuttoning her coat. "I am sorry to hear that. But you're right, that does sound like a good article, Mr. Hoffmeyer. Best of luck with it." Back at her inside office door, she paused and turned back to the reporter.

"Mr. Hoffmeyer—watch your back."

He was no longer smiling. The two understood one another. "I will. I am," he said solemnly. "You do the same." Pulling on a knitted cap that he extricated from a coat pocket, he added, "I left my card with Ms. Torres. You call me anytime, Doctor. You and I should keep in touch."

He went for the door then stopped, reapplying the smile that he had misplaced. "Oh, and great book, by the way! Should have brought my copy with. Had you sign it. Goodbye, Doctor Montgomery. Thanks for hearing me out."

He left. Angel and Donovan met eyes. "Book? I wrote a book? Oh, right!" Donovan joked as she disappeared behind her office door.

Taking off her coat, she considered the unfortunate bit of exposition she had just been given. Eugene Hoffmeyer wasn't there so much to solicit her input on a story as he was to make sure she knew what was happening. Being a smart man, he reached out to the most inside, hooked-up badass he could think of.

She sincerely hoped that he didn't come up butchered or worse before that story of his came out. Odds were good that the two jurors who were now dead were the only two who had been paid off for that not guilty verdict; one would have sufficed, two was just insurance. Somebody needed to check into it. Somebody needed to figure out who had bought them off. But it couldn't be Donovan, not right then. Right then she had to find Bob Lynch.

At her desk, she flipped open the laptop and powered it on. Accessing criminal records using her forensic clearance, she pulled up Bob Lynch's jacket. He had one, and it was impressive: assault with a deadly weapon, drug trafficking, and attempted murder standing out among other lesser criminal pursuits. The botched kidnapping of a real estate tycoon had landed him a five-year incarceration in Menard Correctional, a maximum-security prison in Chester, Illinois.

Maybe Bob Lynch was nothing more than a casual acquaintance, but his rap sheet listed so many shared interests, it was easy to imagine that he and Mason Ghetz would make the best of friends.

According to his file, he owned an auto body shop and was married to a woman named Donna. Donovan considered going to the body shop, but the chances of Bob Lynch engaging in a conversation with her were slim to none. She knew that. And talking to anybody else at the shop might flag her unnecessarily if, indeed, he was more intimately connected to Ghetz.

The file gave a short list of Lynch's white supremacist affiliations, most notably the Aryan Brotherhood. Authorities were later able to assess that he had held the position of a commissioner for that gang while in prison.

By the eighties, the AB had adopted a military-like leadership structure comprised of a twelve-man council that took orders and then implemented those orders, from an elected three-man commission. Donovan knew about this structure, having counseled former members. She knew that even a former commissioner would hold a certain amount of leverage within his gang community. A warped sense of respect for this lofty position could get a great many mountains moved, should he call in that chip. A former commissioner could have people killed with one phone call. He could alter verdicts and sweep away the evidence.

Her mind raced through the possibilities that the information offered. *If* she obtained solid proof that Ghetz and Lynch were somehow in league with one another, that *might* explain why Ghetz walked so easily, cleared of all four murders and back on the street. And *if* Alfredo's hunch was on target and the two men were in bed with one another literally as well as figuratively—well, that would explain everything.

She clicked onto a couple of the group's websites and could see that nothing they had to offer would get her any closer to her target. She would have to find a back door, an alternative approach. Donna Lynch was the answer.

She went to Facebook and pulled up every Donna Lynch, then rooted around on each page to narrow down the list to those in Chicago. Thankfully, the woman Donovan was searching for listed her marital status and husband's name, which expedited the hunt.

The woman's page was active and offered a great deal of information about her. Donovan could certainly glean something here that she needed, whatever it turned out to be. Unfortunately, she would have to go deep-sea diving through myriad posts and albums to find it.

The first dozen posts consisted of banal musings and photos of food. Donovan could have read further but decided to dig into the photo albums instead. She took a brief walk through Donna's childhood and college days, then came upon a photo of her wedding reception showing a young Donna and Bob with a caption that read, "Bob with hair! Look at that mustache!" This was followed by several emoticons of various hearts.

The wedding had taken place in the midseventies, Donovan assessed, by the polyester pastel-colored dresses on the bridesmaids and the fat bowties and baby-blue tuxes on the groomsmen. In the picture, the couple was cutting their three-tiered wedding cake on a long collapsible table covered with a pink-and-white paper tablecloth. They were at a VFW lodge surrounded by paneled walls and a small stage behind them with the VFW emblem hanging above it. The stage was flanked by an American flag on one side and a confederate flag on the other. "Talk to me, Donna," Donovan said aloud to the screen.

Other photos captured Christmas mornings, Thanksgiving dinners, trips to Las Vegas, the birth of a child, and so on. As Donovan studied the photos, she realized two features about Donna Lynch had not changed since college—namely her long, bedazzled nails and lacquered-in-place bleached-blonde hair. The lady spent some serious time in the salon.

Donovan thought she had passed over a post showing a photo of a hand, presumably Donna's, displaying long, squared-off nails painted a bright coral-pink with small rhinestones set in the polish along the nail tips.

What initially hadn't seemed worth her time took on fresh importance. She went back to relocate the post.

"Bingo," Donovan whispered, reading the caption under the found photograph. It read, "Look at these beauties! Pretty Baby is the ONLY place to go for this kind of *pizzazz!*"

She left Facebook and googled the Pretty Baby nail salon. As it turned out, this old-school establishment was located in Gage Park and served as both beauty parlor and nail salon, providing one-stop-shopping for Donna's notable nails and colossal hairdo.

Donovan knew Bob wasn't going to talk to her. Odds were good that Donna wouldn't either. But—maybe her manicurist would. She called the salon and asked if she could get an appointment with whomever did Donna Lynch's nails. She told her that she had just met Donna at a friend's house, was completely taken with her manicure, and had asked where she got them done. She remembered the salon but hadn't gotten the manicurist's name. The woman at the desk was delighted with the question and informed Donovan that the manicurist's name was Nancy.

"Is she in? Do you take walk-ins?" Donovan asked, practically chirping into the phone. The answers were yes and yes.

"Oh, that's great! But I don't know when I can get in there. How late will Nancy be available today?"

"Well, honey, I'm afraid Nance has to leave early today. Her youngest is turning ten. She has to pick up the cake, and, well, you know, all that fun stuff. She's gonna be leaving here no later than four thirty, I think she said."

Donovan thanked her but knew that she probably couldn't get there in time. She promised to consult her calendar and make an actual appointment with Nancy in a couple of days.

"Any time, hon. Any friend of Donna's …"

When the call ended, she noted the time. It was 3:20. Gage Park was fifteen miles and a good hour from Lincoln Square at that time of day. She had just enough time to get there before Nancy left to pick up that birthday cake.

Donovan came flying out of her office, buttoning her coat. "Hey! What's up?" Angel asked.

"Gone for the day, Angie," Donovan answered. "I gotta get my nails done."

Chapter Fifteen

Gage Park was not the most progressive neighborhood in Chicago, but it had graduated away from the white street gangs and Nazi clubs that once held court throughout the area. Known for housing a predominantly Caucasian population, it had, in recent years, grown more ethnically diverse. Brethren of the Ku Klux Klan were no longer comfortable throwing back their hoods and relaxing amid neighbors who shared their same sentiments. They may have still been there, but their agenda of racial, religious, and LGBT intolerance had been begrudgingly forced back underground.

Donovan was aware of Gage Park's sordid past and more equitable present and found the small houses and corner markets to be quaint, if not dated. She even passed a bus bench with a black realtor's face and number painted on it. Things could change, *sometimes.*

Pretty Baby Hair and Nails was easy to find. It stood alone with large address numbers painted over the front door. The sign on the glass of the door was concerning, thought the doctor. It showed a rendering of a chubby baby, circa 1950, naked and posed on her tummy, smiling into a hand mirror that she held while fluffing her curly blonde hair with the other chubby little hand. "At least they didn't paint on acrylic nails," Donovan said to herself as she pulled into the parking lot behind the shop.

Donovan sat in her car, which was pointed toward the back door. A young white woman leaned against the end of the outside wall of the salon smoking a cigarette. She had a dainty nose and full lips with large green eyes that shimmered like jewels against her olive skin and long, black hair. Still, Donovan saw something else on the young woman's face, something—broken. She wore a pink salon smock unbuttoned over black slacks and a turtleneck sweater.

No name on the smock. Early twenties. Just lit a second cigarette, so she's not in a hurry to get back inside. Not a stylist. Working as a salon helper tending to the towels, sweeping up the hair around each chair between customers, maybe taking some calls. She can put up with it for another year while she finishes cosmetology school and gets her license.

This was Donovan's internal monologue as she waited, a profiling game she played with herself to pass the time, a game she never lost.

As Donovan sat behind the wheel, the young woman glanced over at the Prius several times. "Perhaps she's playing a similar game," Donovan mused.

At 4:20, a tall white woman sporting a blonde soccer-mom bob and large hoop earrings came out the back door. She had on a puffy grey nylon jacket and leopard print stretch pants.

"Janice, will you make sure that the laundry gets picked up, honey? I don't think they picked up last night. Hard to keep a nice shop with dirty towels," she called out to the young woman as she started for the parking lot. The young woman exhaled smoke into the air, smiling and nodding. "Sure thing, Nancy. No problem," she responded. The tall woman tossed her a cursory goodbye while fishing for her keys.

Donovan, confident that she had found Nancy, leaped from the car and approached as nonchalantly as she could. In a voice unlike her own—higher, more animated—she introduced herself to the woman. "Hi! Darn it, I'll bet you're Nancy. I tried so hard to get here earlier, but you know how it goes. I'm Jessica, Jessica Tucker. I called earlier. I'm a friend of Donna's."

The woman stopped abruptly, staring at Donovan. By the expression on her face, one might have thought Donovan had just shat herself. "No, you're not a friend of Donna's," she said slowly with ice in her words. "Who are you?"

Donovan knew at once that this was going to be harder than she thought. She countered the woman's venom with more chirping blather.

"Well, I'm not a close friend of hers, not yet. But we met at a party last week, and I asked her where she got those gorgeous nails of hers done. She's such a sweetheart, isn't she? Anyway, I had to try and get in here to see if I could get you to work your magic on me! Nobody but Nancy will do. That's what she told me."

Bending so as to get up in Donovan's face directly, eye to eye, she said, "I don't know who you are, but you're lying. Donna has never been to a party where somebody like you would be on the guest list."

The woman was so aggressively hostile, Donovan knew that nothing she could say would soften her into a conversation. It had been her experience that when racism wasn't coated with even a small amount of sugar, no negotiations would ensue. She decided to cut her losses and bow out of this particular gateway to Bob Lynch as gracefully as she could. "I'm not sure what you mean by that, but I apologize for taking up your time." She spoke softly and sincerely, then started to walk back to her car.

"Hey!" the woman shouted. Donovan turned around.

"Who are you, and how do you know Donna?"

Donovan had to think fast. "I am Jessica Tucker. My friends call me Jessie." Then she took on an embarrassed sort of stance and continued.

"Look—she was at a restaurant last week, okay? A restaurant where I wait tables. I overheard the guy she was with call her by name. They were talking about this place, that she had an appointment with you, how much she loved you, that sort of stuff. That's all. I just thought her nails were so amazing that it would be cool to get mine done like that too. I didn't mean anything by it. You just do really beautiful work."

That was more lies than Donovan had strung together consecutively for longer than she could remember. And it wasn't her best work. If the woman asked what restaurant or why she couldn't just make an appointment, Donovan was going to have to scramble.

The woman stood up straight, swiveling her jaw as she thought through the information she had just been given. After a brief silence, she went back to fishing for her keys in her purse as she spoke.

"I'm not sure I believe that either. You don't look like a waitress to me. Lucky for you, I'm running late." She finally excavated a huge tangle of keys from her large purse and again regarded the doctor.

"But here's something I am sure of," she said, her index finger extended. "You made a wrong turn getting here. Now, if I were you, God forbid, I would get back out of this whole neighborhood just as fast as I could. Understand? Gonna get dark pretty soon, and once it gets dark, you are going to be a lot harder to see. And with all those speeding cars out there, well, something bad might happen to you."

And with that thinly veiled insult masked as advice, she got in her car and pulled out of the lot.

Donovan stood still for a moment. Then she rolled her head from side to side in an effort to relax her neck muscles. *This Mason Ghetz business must be weighing on me more than I realize*, she thought. *I knew that this was a long shot, and I approached that gal just as sloppily as I possibly could. Shame on me.*

Again she started for her car, but this time the young smoking woman stopped her from leaving. It was a whispered shout, as if she didn't want anyone else to hear her. "Hey," she said, nodding her head one time to the left, then walked around the far side of the building facing the alley. Donovan followed.

"Yes, can I help you?" Donovan asked, now a few feet from the girl.

"I heard you asking about Mrs. Lynch."

"Yeah. Yeah, I thought I'd get my nails done by her manicurist, but it seems she—isn't taking new clients right now."

The girl smiled at Donovan's irony, dropped her smoke, and butted it out with her shoe.

The smile let Donovan know that she was on safer turf now. "You know Donna?"

"She's been coming in here for a long time, long before I started working here. I've only been here for a couple of months."

The young woman paused. Donovan could see that she was weighing what next to say. Allowing her that time, she waited.

After an awkward moment, she said, "I'm Janice, Janice Anderson. Six more months before I get my license and my own station. Meanwhile, I'm an assistant here for the whole shop. I'm here a lot, and I hear a lot."

Again, she paused. Again, Donovan waited.

Giving up on graceful pretense, the girl lit another cigarette and laid down her cards. "Okay, I don't know what you're really looking for, but—depending on the question—I may or may not have the answer."

She took a nervous drag and immediately exhaled, staring pensively at Donovan. It was a look Donovan had seen on a number of faces over a number of years. She fished out a twenty from her wallet and handed it to the girl. The girl glanced at the bill. "It's hard to remember everything, but …" Donovan fished out another twenty, and the girl stuck the money in the pocket of her smock.

"Donna Lynch and her very creepy-looking husband Bob have one of those pretend marriages, a marriage of convenience, I think it's called. You know, when people get married because it benefits them both in some way, not because they love each other."

Donovan shook her head affirmatively. "Yes, I've heard the expression."

"Well, it's a known fact that Mr. Lynch keeps another lover, and he has since before they got married."

Just when Donovan had been about to abort her Gage Park adventure, ready to concede that this time her instincts had been misguided, she was being handed the very information she had come for. And it seemed that Bob Lynch might be worth the effort after all.

"Do you know who that person is, Janice?" Donovan softly asked.

The girl stared at her. Donovan rephrased the question.

"Do you know who *the other man* is?"

The girl smiled. "I don't know his name, but I saw him one time. He came in to pick up Mrs. Lynch. He was standing at the door, and Mrs. Lynch said to Nancy, 'Nancy, this is Bob's *special friend* I told you about.' Mrs. Lynch tells Nancy everything. And she doesn't think too much of her husband or his *special friend*, if you know what I mean. She's always high on Oxy and gin. She don't give a shit what she says half the time. Pardon my French."

"I'm fluent myself," Donovan said.

The girl laughed. "Wouldn't that be nice, to have a buttload of money and just stay high all the time?"

Donovan smiled. Something about the girl made the doctor feel strangely protective toward her. There was something in her eyes, something scared and slightly unhinged. Her beauty and youth couldn't hide it, at least not from Donovan.

Pulling up a picture of Mason Ghetz on her phone, the doctor turned the screen toward her charming informant.

"Yeah, that's him. God, he's as creepy looking as Bob Lynch. Those two were meant for each other. Look at that dye job. And that tooth! Hey, why do you want to know this stuff?"

Donovan put her phone in her purse. "I have a better question. Why were you willing to talk to me?"

The girl's face momentarily lost its expressiveness. Every muscle unclenched, as soft and empty as death.

"Because just like you, I don't belong here, but nobody's figured that out yet. If they do, I'll be needing another job, in another state, if I make it out at all. My name's not Janice Anderson. My name is Effie Johnson. I'm passing."

Donovan was humbled silent for a moment. Effie continued.

"And I know who you are. I got a TV. Stay here for a second so nobody sees us leave this alley together, okay?" Donovan nodded as Effie disappeared around the corner of the building. "Hope you find what you're looking for, Doctor Montgomery, but you need to listen to what Nancy said, now. You need to get out of here."

Chapter Sixteen

The impromptu trip to Pretty Baby Hair and Nails, which initially seemed to be nothing more than an awkward exercise in futility, had paid off handsomely for Donovan. Not only was Bob Lynch a person of note when it came to Mason Ghetz, but he was also his lover and had been for decades. Effie Johnson had confirmed it all, and then some. A black girl passing for white, she was as good at keeping secrets as she was at divulging them.

Things were starting to add up in Donovan's mind. Lynch and Ghetz had spent decades underground keeping their relationship buried so as to stay active participants in a white nationalist movement that grew more powerful every day. To be outed would have gotten them ostracized—and killed. Homosexuality was not tolerated by the Aryan Brotherhood; it was stated in the by-laws.

The possibility that Lynch was the one who had put up (or gathered up) the money for Bell Dean, Sally Jones, and a couple of now-dead jurors made perfect sense. That he was behind the mass shooting in an effort to keep Donovan from testifying—and that had the added benefit of sowing chaos and fear in the Black community and law enforcement, both—seemed equally logical. Plus, he could have gotten those specifics to happen without lifting a finger. The prestige and respect extended to him by virtue of having served as an AB commissioner while serving time in Menard meant that if he wanted it done—it got done. If Mason

173

Ghetz was that important to the Brotherhood, as Bob Lynch may well have suggested he was, no questions would be asked.

Donovan would find out if that was the case, but she had a couple of plans to carry out first.

Buttoning her trench coat against a mounting chill in the air, she exited the alley and quickly scooted into her car after allowing the young woman enough time to get back inside the shop. She believed she had been given good advice by both the manicurist and shop intern; get out of Gage Park ASAP. Besides, it was getting late and she had a great deal to accomplish before the day was through.

Her next stop would be the Temple office building across from Daley Plaza where, little more than a week prior, someone with an AR-15 sat perched at a window on the twenty-first floor aiming to kill her. Instead, thirty-two other people had died. She intended to find out who had pulled the trigger.

As she made her way through traffic, she turned on the radio. News volleyed between the mass shooting, exoneration of Mason Ghetz, and the upcoming congressional election that included a neo-Nazi candidate among the names on the ballot. That election would be taking place in two weeks. Given the outcome of the Ghetz trial and division among Chicagoans regarding the verdict, the possibility of an openly declared neo-Nazi gaining the seat seemed less fantastical than it might have at other times.

Donovan turned the radio off.

She entered InterPark on West Washington, found a space, and took off on foot. She stood in front of the Chicago Temple Building, then decided to cross the street and study the structure from Daley Plaza.

The architecturally stunning building, erected in 1924, was, at the time of its completion, the tallest building in Chicago. A tourist must-see, its twenty-three stories contained three spiritual sanctuaries: the main Methodist church on the first floor, the Dixon Chapel on the second, and the Sky Chapel that occupied the twenty-third floor more than four hundred feet above the ground. The Methodist church's senior pastor was the only residential tenant. His apartment and other things "chapel" monopolized the rest of the twenty-third as well as twenty-second floors. Everything in between was dedicated to commercial office space.

As Donovan craned her neck back to take in the entirety of the edifice, she remembered reading that the distance from the sidewalk to the cross atop the gothic-inspired steeple was greater than that of the Washington Monument. She took in the magnificence of the steeple, then the ominously boarded-over window a few floors below.

She stared up, contemplating the strategy of the shooter, or whomever had hired the shooter. There were so many other ways to target her, from her daily arrival to and departure from her office to any number of errands she ran on a regular basis. Still, if seeming randomness was the shooter's goal, this was a better vantage point. But—the people there that day, the associates gathered around her could have been targets as well. State's Attorney Jen Park, even Jordan, might have added impressive kills for "Team Ghetz." That made better sense to her; she was the target, but her company sweetened the deal and made taking this particular chance from that window quite attractive.

As she pondered the shooter's intentions, a woman approached her. She was holding a dog leash with a small French bulldog at the end of it.

"Unbelievable, isn't it?" said the woman. She stood next to Donovan, also gazing up at the Temple Building. "Thirty-five people shot from right there." She referred to the covered twenty-first-story window. Donovan glanced at the woman, then back at the window.

"Thirty-two," she gently corrected her.

"Was it?" said the woman, glancing at Donovan, then back at the window. "Seemed like a million. What a nightmare. I can hardly bring myself to walk through here now. All those horrible images the news keeps showing of all those poor people. Right here! Right here in Daley Plaza. This is where Buddy and I have always taken our evening constitutional, every day, rain or shine. Now I feel like I'm walking through a graveyard."

Donovan regarded the woman, thinking how impacted the city at large had been by this hideous deed. Being so focused on the nuts and bolts of the crime, she had not considered the bloodstain covering Chicago, still wet to the touch, too set in to ever be washed away.

The woman paused as if having a revelation of some kind. She studied Donovan, then squinted her eyes as if that might make her see better. "Say, don't I know you?" she said with a friendly clip to her voice. "You work around here?" Buddy, the French bulldog, wagged his tail and butted Donovan's leg with his head.

The doctor bent to give him a pet. "Sometimes. Maybe we've passed one another in the plaza," she offered with a smile.

All at once, the woman's expression changed as she registered from where she had seen Donovan Montgomery. Donovan stopped petting Buddy and stood up. She clearly read the woman's internal monologue. Maybe she was projecting her own critique onto the woman, but Donovan could hear each word as if she were speaking aloud. *It was you. You're the reason that brute isn't in jail. You're the villain, the enemy. Just another attention-grabbing media hound, that's all you are.*

Without so much as a "bye-bye," she gave her furry friend a small yank and retreated. Instinctively following in his master's footsteps, the dog yapped disapprovingly at Donovan before turning his attention to the concrete in front of him.

"Everybody's a fucking critic," Donovan said, moving toward the street on her way to the Temple Building. As she started across, she saw Detective DuMont in a squad car parked illegally near the front door.

She turned and stepped back into the plaza, practically jogging toward the Picasso. She tucked herself behind the sculpture, then turned to face the Temple Building. The squad car was still there.

He suspects I'm responsible for the three dead bodies they hauled out of the Satin Door, she thought. *Well, if you think you're going to stay glued to my tail until you have some proof, that's not gonna work out, Detective. I have work to do.* As she watched DuMont pull away from the curb and take off down Washington at a slow roll, she reconsidered.

Running into him twice the day after the nightclub incident could be nothing more than an uncomfortably sticky coincidence. There were plenty of reasons for him to be casing the building and surrounding area. He, too, was trying to figure out who had shot all of those people. The good news was that seeing him produced an appreciated double shot of adrenaline in her. Donovan knew that she would need to get to the bottom of things soon if she was going to wrap it up herself. The entire Chicago police force was working on the same task.

But this was hers.

There were too many eyes on her and too much recognition. Thankfully, Buddy's owner had reminded her of that. If she was going to gather the information she wanted from the Temple Building, she needed to protect her anonymity.

Donovan sat on the stone frame that surrounded the Chicago Picasso facing away from the street. Taking out a makeup case from her clutch, she extracted a powder compact and small plastic box. It held a tiny piece of rubber that transformed her button nose to one with a more pronounced bridge. Employing the two-sided tape on the prosthetic and finesse that she had acquired in applying it, she skillfully worked the rubber over her nose with one hand, holding the open compact in the other. The compact gave her both a mirror and a powder base to finish the job. Next, she slid on a pair of oversized, eighties-esque glasses housing nonprescription lenses. The glass did not impede her vision but was cut thick enough to alter the appearance of her eyes. The size of the glasses gracefully covered most of the prosthetic's edges. She then pulled her hair back and threw on a scrunchie that she carried for such occasions. This had long been her go-to disguise, and one that she could manage at a moment's notice.

With her appearance slightly altered, she crossed the street, approaching the neo-Gothic white marble walls of 77 West Washington. She entered through the large glass doors trimmed with shimmering bronze that opened into the Temple Building's venerable lobby.

She stepped slowly into the marbled corridor along a highly polished tile floor. At the end of the lobby, past a stretch of bronze elevator doors and wall sconces, a directory hung behind glass in a shimmering metal case. Donovan had been in this building many times, but its impact was not lessened by familiarity. It remained one of Chicago's most impressive and well-preserved treasures. But she wasn't moving slowly to take in the ambiance. She was checking for security cameras.

The iconic building maintained much of its original early-twenties charm. Security cameras tucked in every corner could arguably sully the aesthetic. There were none as far as Donovan could see. That didn't mean they weren't there. She would proceed as if they were.

A small group of people waited for someone to join them before entering the Methodist church on the first floor. Two men in business suits got off an elevator and headed toward the doors Donovan had just entered. She saw a maintenance man mopping the floor at the end of the long corridor just past the directory sign. He saw her noticing him and mopped more slowly, staring her down in what Donovan perceived as an aggressive kind of way. *What's that about?* she wondered. *Everybody's still a little on edge around here, I suppose.*

The people in the Chicago Temple Building moved about as if everything was normal, as if someone hadn't walked among them with the intention of slaughtering a bunch of innocent people, but no one was quite able to pull it off. The horror of what took place on the twenty-first floor hung in the air, thick and dark.

In that building were clues as to what had happened up there. Maybe a guy off the street had come in with a cache of weapons and ammunition unnoticed. Maybe. But it would be an easier task to accomplish if it had been organized from the inside. Donovan knew that and intended to visit the Maintenance Department. She wanted to ask a few questions.

A large African American security guard approached her just as she started for an elevator. Unlike a doughy department store security guard, this man was muscular with broad shoulders and a 10mm Glock holstered at his side. "Sorry, miss. But we've been asked to have everybody sign in since the shooting." He extended a clipboard and a pen. "And I need to see a photo ID, too. Sorry."

Donovan took the clipboard. "Of course. I understand," she said, signing in as Jessica Tucker, the same name she had given the manicurist. Then she took out her wallet and handed him Jessica Tucker's driver's license, which showed a photo of Donovan. Not being one to overlook details, she had on her go-to disguise in the photo. This fake ID had come in handy on more than one occasion. It had been a gift from an ex-client who owed her a favor.

"Thank you, miss," he said as he took the ID, glancing back and forth between it and the lady in front of him. She smiled. He smiled back while handing her the ID. As she gave him the board and pen, he asked, "Can I help you find something?"

"Yes, actually, you can," she responded warmly. "Where would I find the maintenance office? I'm working for a building contractor, and the company is interested in speaking with the maintenance company about taking on their contract."

He shook his head and bit his lip. "Let me … Hold on a sec." He lifted the walkie-talkie from his belt and contacted someone. After a brief exchange, he returned the device and addressed Donovan directly.

"I guess they don't want folks using the freight elevators as a rule. So, they said for you to take one of these elevators down to the basement and then get on the freight elevator there. That will take you down to sub-basement two, miss." He smiled again. "I've only been stationed here for a few days. Still learning the lay of the land."

Donovan thanked him and moved toward the elevators. As she waited for one of the ornate doors to open, she saw the sullen maintenance man still mopping at the end of the corridor around the corner from the directory sign. She turned and involuntarily made eye contact with him. He broke their gaze, placing his mop into a large bucket on rollers at his feet.

As he bent to grab the handle of the supply cart, Donovan saw a faint tattoo on his neck peeking out from the collar of his maintenance coveralls. It depicted a shamrock with two zigzag lightning bolts reminiscent of swastikas superimposed over it, and Donovan recognized it as an Aryan symbol she had seen on some of the gang members she had counseled. *Okay,* she thought.

Once in the elevator, she pushed the button for the twenty-first floor. Making every effort to appear like she knew exactly where she was, she walked with purpose, passing a businessman moving in the opposite direction. A few wrong turns and several hallways later, she arrived at her destination. Yellow police tape covered the door in a large X, repeating the admonition that she must not enter.

She glanced around and saw no one. Tightening her black leather gloves securely around her fingers, gloves that had been so helpful to her over the past forty-eight hours, she cautiously peeled back the tape and jimmied the lock on the office door with a nail file from her clutch.

Whatever she thought she could glean from this break-in would have to be gathered quickly. The yellow tape hanging loose and impotent to either side of the doorframe would scream like a siren at midnight should another businessperson come down that hall. Some were gone for the day by then, but because people kept a wide variety of hours, she could not count on luck to constantly bail her out.

As she stood in the dark office, she could feel a presence, like eyes on her from somewhere hidden. She checked the ceiling for cameras and saw none. Donovan had never been prone to believing in anything "other-worldly," but as she took two more steps farther in, she could feel them; she could even see them both.

First, she saw Saul Jacobson sitting at his desk. He exchanged words with the man holding the gun who would have been standing right where Donovan stood. Then before he could make a good argument for his life, part of his skull landed on his desk. Perhaps he saw it on the blotter before his head dropped forward.

Then, Hannah Bird, the cleaning woman, knocked. "Maintenance, Mr. Jacobson. It's Hannah. May I come in?" she asked from the other side of the door, though she had no intention of not entering. Announcing herself was just a respectful formality that she and the businessman exchanged regularly, as he often worked late and would be there when she came in to empty the trash cans. But she didn't get to the trash cans.

She opened the door and saw the gentleman seated and motionless at his blood-soaked desk. As her brain tried to make sense of what she was seeing, a man stepped in front of her and shot Hannah between the eyes at close range before she had too much time to panic and no time to scream.

Donovan glanced over at the spot where the bodies had been dragged, blood tracks marking where they had been when they were murdered and where they were deposited moments later. Then she checked the window that was boarded from the outside. The precision of the cut in the glass was impressive—and small.

All this, she thought. *All this for that.*

She realized she had gathered no further information, nothing that would get her any closer to Ghetz or Lynch, not by being in that office, anyway, and turned to leave.

She pivoted just in time to watch the office door slowly open. Knowing that she was about to be fingered as the one who broke into the sealed-off room, she quickly considered her options: hide or start talking. Before deciding, a cleaning woman poked her head into the room.

The woman used a white dust rag to push the door open so as to not touch it with her hand and only opened it wide enough to show Donovan the upper part of her face. The two were frozen in their respective places staring at one another. The woman's eyes were cartoonishly large as if she had just seen a ghost. In that Donovan wasn't too sure that she, herself, hadn't just visited the two souls who had been murdered there, she understood the look.

"You get out. You get out of that room right now," the woman whispered urgently. "Who are you? You ain't supposed to be in there. Nobody is," she continued as Donovan met her at the door, guiding them both out into the middle of the hallway.

Donovan masterfully recovered the door with the dangling tape, making sure it was securely stuck to all four corners. With a smile and embarrassed expression on her face, she said, "I'm so sorry. I—I actually just got lost up here. Innocent mistake. I'm trying to get to the maintenance office. I'm working for a building contractor, and the company is interested in speaking with the maintenance company about taking on their contract."

"The maintenance office? On sublevel two?" the woman asked incredulously. "That was some wrong turn, lady. How did you get yourself *in* there?" When she gestured to the taped-off room, she shivered visibly.

Now standing in the hallway, Donovan took a long, hard look at the cleaning woman who had inadvertently complicated her evening. She appeared to be in her forties, maybe fifties with dark brown skin, hair, and eyes. Her hair showed no signs of grey, but that could have been achieved by investing in any eight-dollar box of drugstore dye. Her fragility was what made her seem older to Donovan. The name on her name tag read Beth Ann.

If Donovan excused herself and walked away, the woman would probably contact security. She might just shake it off, but the expression on her face suggested that calling security was already on her mind. And if she did, that would impact Donovan's plans even more dramatically. The woman appeared kind and scared. Donovan chose to seize the opportunity.

The doctor relaxed her shoulders. "Beth Ann. That's pretty. A very Midwestern name. You from Illinois, Beth Ann?"

Donovan watched the woman calculating whether to answer her or report her. The cleaning woman did neither, hurriedly grabbing the handle of her pushcart with every intention of getting away from Donovan and the yellow tape as quickly as possible.

"Beth Ann," Donovan said again before the woman had made her escape. Beth Ann stopped and gave Donovan her best steely glare, allowing her indignation and impatience to speak for her. Donovan saw the anxiety radiating behind the woman's annoyance.

"Beth Ann," she said again, stepping nearer to the woman, closing the distance between them. "Who was working the floor that night, the night before the shooting?"

Beth Ann's face went ashy. All faux emotions were flushed away with that one question, leaving the only emotion she really felt: fear. It came up off her like steam from a radiator that was about to bust. She loosened her grip on the pushcart and faced Donovan directly, trying her best to act as though she weren't afraid for her life.

"I don't remember, miss … What did you say your name was?"

"My name is Jessica Tucker," Donovan said warmly, hoping to put the woman at ease.

"Well, I'm Beth Ann Washington, and I didn't see anything." She spoke as if she had rehearsed the line. "You ain't really looking for the Maintenance Department, are you, Miss Tucker?"

Donovan could see where this was going. Beth Ann was afraid of someone or several people in that department. She couldn't talk to Donovan freely, and she couldn't afford to *not* talk to her on the outside chance that she was being monitored to make sure she was keeping her mouth shut.

"Yes, Beth Ann," Donovan quietly said. "I am headed for the Maintenance Department. But I don't work for them. I promise you. I wanted to see the room first."

She shook her head slowly. "What do you want with this place?"

"Answers. Beth Ann, were there any men assigned to this floor that night?"

"Women clean out the offices; the men clean the bathrooms."

Playing a hunch that Beth Ann knew the cleaning woman who was murdered in the room, Donovan took a chance, hoping to push the right button. "Did you know Hannah Bird?" she asked.

Beth Ann's brow wrinkled as she bit her lip. "My best friend," she managed to choke out.

"Well, out of respect for her, Beth Ann, who was here that night?"

"Charlie was the regular guy, but he was sick that night. Somebody filled in for him, but I didn't see who it was."

Donovan got up in Beth Ann's face, gently laying her gloved hand over the cleaning woman's, which was resting on the handle of the pushcart.

"I think you did," Donovan said.

Beth Ann began to slowly shake her head no as tears filled her warm, troubled eyes.

"You haven't seen Charlie since he fell ill, have you?"

She continued shaking her head.

"I think you and I are pretty sure Charlie's dead now, aren't we?"

A tear rolled down the woman's face, followed by another.

"Lady, I don't know what you're looking for, but you need to get out of here or I'm gonna call my boss." She reached for her cell phone. Donovan grabbed her wrist. The physical gesture startled the woman. She tried to pull away but couldn't.

Before she screamed, Donovan whispered in her ear, "Look, I can't explain everything to you right now, but I'm a good guy, okay? I'm a good guy, and there are some very bad guys trying to kill me. Just like they killed Charlie. Just like they killed Hannah. So, sister, please—*please* think. Who worked this floor that night?"

Everything about the woman changed at that moment. This mysterious stranger sneaking into forbidden places, this trespasser might turn out to be an avenging angel, an ally. Beth Ann needed an ally. She wiped the tears from her cheeks.

"He works for maintenance. He's the regional manager. Oversees twenty buildings. He's a very powerful man. Saw him that night on this floor. Saw him turn that corner. He didn't see me. Thank you, Jesus." She started to tear up again. "Not in my darkest nightmare could I have imagined … Poor Hannah. Poor little thing."

"Thank you, Beth Ann. Thank you. You just made it right. Yes, you did."

Donovan took a step back, sliding her hands in the pockets of her trench coat as Beth Ann studied her. "Mm-hmm. Well, whoever you are, you do the same."

Donovan watched Beth Ann push her supply cart down the long corridor. A man came out of an office at the far end. He appeared to be leaving for the day in a coat with a briefcase tucked under his arm. He made no eye contact as he moved toward the elevator.

"Down this hall to the left," Beth Ann called out in normal, conversational tones.

"What is?" Donovan asked.

"The freight elevator. That'll take you all the way down to the maintenance offices. They'll be able to help you with that contract of yours. You'll see it. Right next to where the loading docks are. Right there on sub-basement two." She smiled and spoke in full voice. "You just got lost, that's all. Happens all the time. Take care now."

She stopped smiling and nodded her head at the doctor before disappearing from view.

Chapter Seventeen

If Donovan were to believe in miracles, finding Beth Ann would have constituted a big one. Of course, Beth Ann had found *her*, which made the whole encounter that much more providential.

The man who had killed Saul Jacobson, Hannah Bird, the regular maintenance man Charlie, and thirty-two other equally innocent people worked for maintenance, a regional manager who took care of twenty buildings. Beth Ann seemed to think he was a very powerful man. Donovan was in the perfect mood to find out.

At the end of the hall, before she reached the freight elevator, she made a mental note of the last office on the right. The lettering on the door read Gottlieb and Gottlieb Liturgical Music. "Gonna need that," she said softly.

Approaching the elevator, she recalled another powerful man who had monopolized the media for a few days. That was some time ago. Donovan tried to remember exactly when and thought it might have been about three years back. A judge who had made a name for himself in Chicago because of his consistently harsh sentencing was arrested and tried for a string of child killings that took place over a period of two years.

The evidence was strong against him. His whereabouts could be traced to the areas where all three bodies were later found, duct tape and a hunting knife were removed from his trunk, and the blood that the authorities lifted from that knife matched the DNA of the last murdered child. But his prints weren't on it, and none of the bodies held any trace of *his* DNA.

He claimed he had been framed. The jury let him walk. Insufficient evidence, reasonable doubt, and a foothold in the community that had some in awe and others in fear of his wrath managed to get him cleared of all charges.

Four days after the verdict, two kids riding their bikes stopped to explore an abandoned warehouse in Fuller Park on the South Side. There, they found the judge hanging from a rusted overhead crane. He had been hung by his feet, arms secured to his sides with duct tape. *That's right*, Donovan remembered clearly. *It was three years ago.* She could still smell him.

Standing at the freight elevator patiently waiting for the large door to open, she repositioned the faux glasses on her prosthetic nose and checked the time. When the door finally pulled back, it slowly revealed the maintenance man with whom she had locked eyes in the lobby, the sullen man with the tattooed neck.

He stood straight and still with his hands clasped. The supply cart housing the mop and bucket were next to him, and he displayed the same vaguely menacing expression that she had observed on the main floor.

At a glance, he appeared to be expecting her. As she became evident to him standing on the other side of the door, his gaunt face registered no surprise, simply a nonchalant look of obedient insolence like a child following a parent's punishment. But that could not have been the case. He had no way of knowing she would be there—unless someone had seen her.

Did someone see her break into the taped-off suite? Did they see her talking with the cleaning woman? Were there hidden cameras? If the answer to any of those questions was yes, Beth Ann would be in even greater danger than she already was. Donovan filed that possibility in her head and started across the rubber and metal lip of the large steel box.

Before she got on, the sullen man spread his legs a few more inches apart and said, "You need to take the regular elevator to leave the building. This is the freight elevator."

She momentarily considered his advice, then got in the box alongside him, smiling. Unless and until she received some confirmation that she was, indeed, being observed, she would play her hand the way she had anticipated playing it.

"Well," she said, "I'm not leaving the building yet. I just dropped in to say hi to an old client on this floor. I'm actually here to talk with someone in maintenance. I understand that's on sub-basement two?"

The sullen man dropped his "at-attention" stance, stopped the door with his foot and hand, and turned toward her, scowling and cocking his head to one side. His reaction pleased Donovan. He neither forbade her from descending to the sub-basement nor did he attempt to kill her. Odds of her having been observed moments before were looking slim.

"I'm working for a contractor who is just about to lease out some new sites, and he's eager to contract with a maintenance company to take care of them."

He continued to stare at her, unimpressed with this unnecessary personal exposition. "Whatever. Why would I care why you're in the building? You still need to take the regular elevator down to …"

"You know, I've been waiting for the regular elevator for too long. You need to tell somebody about that. Anyway, this door opened. I was supposed to meet with the guy … Oh, where is his name …" She fished around in her clutch bag for a moment. "Anyway, I was supposed to be there thirty minutes ago, so, if you don't mind, I'll take this one, okay?" she said, couching her assertion as a question, then clasped her hands in front of her as he had done and stared while waiting for the large door to close.

He sneered, then acquiesced, removing his foot from the floor sensor in the doorframe and pushed the button for sub-basement two.

Once convinced that the elevator was headed to where she wanted to go, the doctor glanced cautiously sideways at the sullen man. Maintaining the smile on her face, she said, "Thank you." He let out a small moan of frustration under his breath.

Now standing where she could observe the man, Donovan noted another tattoo on the opposite side of his neck. This one depicted a shield inked over two crossed swords. The shield was divided into four sections, each framing a different symbol: a swastika, SS lightning bolts, the letters SB, and a confederate flag. Under this tattoo were the numbers 14/23.

She observed something else; the collar of his maintenance overalls was covered in dark, suntan-colored makeup. Donovan had seen this before. Covering tattoos was common for both men and women attempting to get back into the workforce after doing time, especially if the ink was related to a gang or other nefarious affiliation. Unfortunately, the stuff seemed to always go on thick and greasy like the pancake makeup used in theatre. There was no doubt in her mind that these tattoos had been covered to conceal them from the public, but the sullen man's sweat had betrayed his efforts.

These tattoos told Donovan quite a bit. The one she had seen in the lobby tagged him as a member of the Aryan Brotherhood, the largest white supremacist gang in the world. But he hadn't been in the Brotherhood for long. His tattoo only showed the shamrock and lightning bolts. She knew that as members earned their stripes through beating guards and killing black and Hispanic inmates, they had additional images added to the initial art, such as an eagle, swastika, iron cross, and a red lightning bolt for murder. She also knew that he had not worked there long, as he hadn't yet mastered how to best hide his ink. And based on the tattoo she had observed on the other side of his neck, he had been a member of the Southern Brotherhood, a large white supremacist prison gang based in Alabama. The Southern Brotherhood was an active faction of the Aryan Brotherhood.

There were several white supremacist organizations to choose from. Beyond the Aryan Brotherhood, gangs of note included skinheads, Ku Klux Klan, peckerwoods, and neo-Nazis, among others. Donovan had counseled many former members of these gangs. She also took the stand to help convict many others. It was happenstance that the Southern Brotherhood was as familiar to her as it was. She recognized the shield and its symbols. She knew the meaning of 14/23.

For all white supremacist gangs across the board, the number 14 represented the fourteen words that made up the white supremacist slogan: "We must secure the existence of our people and a future for white children." The twenty-three was for the twenty-three precepts that those who joined the Southern Brotherhood must obey, which included a variety of rules such as not incurring any debt that cannot be repaid and a commitment to not "huff lacquer."

She knew exactly how this man felt about being in an elevator with a black woman who looked like money and sounded like a college degree. And because she knew how much he hated her, she decided to engage him in conversation.

"Horrible what happened in Daley Plaza. Just horrible." She glanced back and forth between the man and the door. His expression remained unchanged and his lips closed. "Must be kind of creepy working here after what happened. You ever get the creeps working here now? Knowing that guy shot all those people from this building?" She stared at him for a long moment, then turned back to the door. "Guns! Somebody has got to do something about the gun epidemic in this country, don't you think? And in a church, of all places! I mean, sure, this building houses lots of other businesses, but ..."

The elevator stopped and the door opened on the third floor, but no one was waiting to get on. He bared his teeth and hit the button again. Donovan fought back a chuckle.

When the door opened next, Donovan read the signage hanging on the wall across from the elevator that pointed in one direction for the loading docks and the opposite direction for the maintenance offices. The sullen man bolted off in one direction, Donovan in the other.

The rubber pads she had applied to the soles of her ankle boots allowed her to move silently as she made her way through the long, unadorned corridor. She liked these boots with her tapered pants tucked inside. A bargain at just under six hundred dollars from Saks, these Jimmy Choos were the same ones she'd had on the night before at the Satin Door. The boots, along with the concrete walkway, brought back the feeling she'd had when being escorted by force down the hall in the club that led to Daryl Hartford's office. Donovan smiled.

Maintenance consisted of two offices, both with long windows that ran the length of each room, both nondescript and utilitarian by design.

In one, the lights were off. In the other, the lights were on, the glass door standing open by means of a built-in kick stop.

Donovan stood at the doorway.

Sitting at the desk closest the door sorting through invoices was Shift Supervisor Craig Apperson, according to the cork and brass sign displayed next to the landline to his left. His sandy-blond hair was combed straight back and held in place by shiny product of some kind. Thin but for a hyperextended midsection, he wore a white quarter-sleeved shirt and fat green tie, and Donovan caught a glimpse of a pocket protector secured over his shirt pocket, a pen visible within.

Another man stood in front of a desk opposite Craig's that was cluttered with files and cardboard boxes. He wore maintenance coveralls. Frowning while riffling through an awkwardly stacked pile of papers in front of him, his small frame seemed to buckle under slumped shoulders. Toward the back of the office sat a third person at a tidy desk. This man wore a suit. He sat huddled over the desktop, elbows resting on the metal surface, studying his cell phone while furiously thump-typing with a mindless half grin on his large, flushed face.

The room smelled of pizza. In the ceiling, one fluorescent tube did the work for two blanketing the area with harsh, unflattering light. A radio sat on a shelf over the desk filled with boxes. It was turned on but barely audible. Donovan could only assess the topic, which was women's rights. She thought she heard the talk show host take a less than favorable position on the matter. The fourth desk sat unmanned with a cheap coffee pot and coffee paraphernalia covering its surface. Two desks faced one wall, and two desks faced the other. *Worst feng shui ever*, thought Donovan.

Nobody turned to look at her. Nobody seemed to know she was there, each fully engrossed in whatever he was doing and oblivious to this unexpected company. After leisurely taking in the surrounding, she gently tapped the glass on the open door.

Craig Apperson whipped around, as did the other two men. Now all three regarded Donovan with a combination of apathy and disdain. "Can we help you?" the shift supervisor asked.

"Hi. Hey, sorry to just pop in like this, but I work for Gottlieb and Gottlieb Liturgical Music up on the twenty-first floor, and we haven't had our trash picked up since the shooting. Is anybody working that floor?"

That should help me pinpoint any white supremacists in the room—a black woman working for Jewish folks. How you like me now? she thought playfully.

The men exchanged looks between them. The man sorting files returned to sorting them, and the man in the suit turned his attention back to his phone. But he only addressed it for a moment, then hit the button on the side and placed it face down on his desk. A shiny American flag sticker on the back of the phone reflected in the fluorescent light, catching Donovan's eye.

The man in the suit stood up and faced Donovan. So did Craig Apperson.

"Uh-huh. Well, yes, we do have a crew taking care of the offices up there. I'll have someone look into it. Is there anything else we can do for you?" His hands were at his sides. The man in the suit had his hands in his pockets. Both attempted to appear imposing in an alpha dog way that Donovan had encountered a million other times.

She grinned and nodded. "No, nothing else. Thanks for checking into it." She turned, giving the impression she was about to leave, then swiveled back around. When she did, her expression had changed to somber, the space between her eyes pinched a little to show concern.

"What a horrible thing, two people killed by some maniac right here in this beautiful building and another thirty-two gunned down by the same monster the next morning." She waited for some response. There was none.

Donovan thought it odd that neither the sullen tattooed man nor any one of these three bothered to throw out even the most banal agreement when confronted with someone talking about the shooting. "Yes, terrible thing" or "Still can't believe it" would have seemed much less suspicious than saying nothing. *Is everyone in the building so self-absorbed that what happened here is really not registering? Or—are they all involved?* she asked herself.

"Well, thanks again," she said, turning to leave. After a moment's pause, she stepped back to the frame of the door.

"Say, as long as I'm down here, are all of your workers bonded? I have a nephew who really needs a job. I think this sort of thing would be perfect for him, but he just got out of jail and employment opportunities are, well, limited for him, poor thing."

Craig Apperson scowled, turning back to his desk. He didn't sit down. He just pushed a stack of papers this way and that, staring at nothing. The man in the suit stepped toward her, attempting to smile. His lips curled upward, but his forehead folded like an accordion. "Why don't you leave your card. If anything opens up, we'll give him a call and set up an interview."

"Thank you!" Donovan gushed. "That's very kind. But I don't keep any business cards. Do you have one?"

The man in the suit moved reluctantly back to his desk and picked up a business card from a card caddy with American flags molded in plastic on both sides. He handed it to her. There was a small photo of the man in the corner of the card. She realized she had been conversing with David Fischer, regional manager. There he stood; the man who had shot all of those people in an attempt to kill Donovan Montgomery had just handed her his business card.

Bingo, she said to herself. *Let the party begin.*

The man who had been sorting through files now had a stack in his arms and left the room, pushing past Donovan. He offered an abbreviated, "Sorry," as he did so. The doctor had been profiling since entering the room, and the man with the files was of no concern to her. He knew nothing. He had no agenda other than whatever had been asked of him regarding that stack of paperwork. But David Fischer was a very bad man with some deplorable associates, and Craig Apperson—time would tell.

"Regional manager! Impressive," she said. "A man like you would be able to take care of my nephew, I do believe. Thanks again."

She opened her clutch and extracted her wallet to stick the card in a safe place. While performing this idle task, she said, "Hey, maybe one of you guys would know. What ever happened to Charlie?"

She finished playing with her purse and casually watched for a reaction.

For a moment, Donovan, Craig, and Dave Fischer stood silently, the shoes of the man with the files softly squeaking as they moved farther away down the hall. The two men appeared angry and confused. Donovan broke the moment.

"I liked Charlie. He wasn't there that night, thank God. I know that. We saw the guy they sent to replace him, but neither Sheila nor I have seen Charlie since. Is he coming back?"

Dave Fischer stepped toward her, and Craig folded his arms across his chest. "You saw the guy?" he asked.

Donovan stayed light and conversational. "Yeah, well, I mean, he was at the far end of the hall. I just saw the back of him, but Sheila, the gal I work with, she saw him. Charlie was just always so sweet and, you know, you get used to certain folks being around. Of course, I wouldn't blame him if he never came back after that. The shooting, you know."

Dave Fischer relaxed his attack stance and took a small step back from the doctor. "Charlie got another job," Craig answered. "He already had it lined up before … before the incident."

She shook her head. "Thank God. Well, we'll miss seeing him around. Were either of you in the building that night?" She gasped in horror at the thought.

Craig Apperson gave Dave Fischer a look that let Donovan know she had definitely outstayed her welcome.

"No," Dave mustered. "No, I was in another building. We have several down here in the Loop. And Craig was off that night." He approached her as he talked, in the hopes of inspiring her to leave. She understood the cue and complied.

"Oh, thank God. I'm so glad to hear it. Thanks again."

Donovan adjusted her glasses and gave a small wave. As she took off down the barren hall, she thought about her amazing good fortune; the business card and the man who had gifted it to her were like a bouquet of roses on opening night.

We are going to do some business, Dave, she promised herself. *We surely are.*

Chapter Eighteen

Donovan had no intention of getting on the elevator before taking a short tour of the loading docks. As she approached the L-shaped area, she passed a pile of empty five-gallon water bottles against one wall. Further down the L were two large, steel-handled platform carts loaded with plastic-lidded bins, and between them were dozens of wooden pallets, one on top of the other. The ceiling was masked by a web of massive pipes, wires, and scaffolding.

Turning at the joint of the L, a long row of canvas bags full of trash lined the wall, some tied closed, some not, followed by five commercial dumpsters. Next to those stood a trash compactor. A huge beast covering about nine feet vertically against one concrete wall, the compactor seemed much newer than the dumpsters or anything else around it. The red paint still shined, the signage attached unscathed by so much as a smudge.

Beyond the bags, dumpsters, and compactor were the docks. There were several, each with fat yellow lines painted around them and the same yellow lines extending from the ports to help guide trucks safely in and out. All but one was open and empty. Dock lights illuminated their vacant insides. That glow, in addition to a few strategically hung bulbs, swinging from the wire web above amply lit the rest of the workspace.

She noted two security cameras positioned above and aimed at the docks, nowhere else. She carefully moved closer to the wall opposite the ports where more pallets and boxes were being stored. There she was sure to have cleared the cameras' reach. Three trucks were parked side by side at the far end.

Because there was no one to be seen around the docks, Donovan had time to connect the dots in her head while taking in the environment. The weapons and ammo used in the shooting that took place from the twenty-first floor could easily have been transported into the building by accessing nothing more exotic than a truck, driver, and industrial dolly. Dave Fischer had all of that at his disposal. As the regional manager of the Maintenance Department, it would have been a simple task. Maybe he took care of everything himself. If he did have help from within the building, that aid would have surely been given without any questions, either out of allegiance to the Brotherhood or because he was the boss.

She thought through the line of progression while tightening the cuffs of her black leather gloves. *So, we know who did it and how he did it. Now, Fischer or one of his lackeys is going to lead me to Lynch, and Lynch to Ghetz. I just need to track down the elusive Mr. Lynch before Detective DuMont beats me to it. Gonna have to go back to that office and try a little harder.*

Wrapping up her internal monologue, she pulled out her phone to check the time and tucked it back in her clutch. "When I find you, Bob, I—gots— Ghetz," she whispered aloud, grinning. "Once we do that, everybody in Chicago can get a good night's sleep."

Donovan returned to maintenance, hoping to carefully extract Lynch's whereabouts without blowing her cover.

There stood David Fischer and the sullen man blocking her path, staring.

They had paused several feet away from her, near the canvas trash bags. She stood near the trucks. Even with the distance between them, Donovan knew she was trapped. She also knew that with one call from Dave Fischer she would be outnumbered in a much more dramatic way. The doctor wasn't sure she could take on an entire pack of wild dogs, not easily. She had a great deal to do and a short amount of time to do it, but right then handling that roadblock of two took precedence over everything else and could not be avoided.

She considered buying more time with the continued charade that she had worked about hoping to land a job for her nephew, though doing so now seemed like an exercise in futility. Besides, it would be easier to find Lynch with these two than without them. Nevertheless, an exit without a scene would be preferable.

The men remained near the bags. Staying tucked close to the wall as she moved forward, she kept an eye on where the cameras were pointed and remained outside that vantage point.

"Hi again," she said, strolling in their direction. "I had an uncle who worked in a place like this. Just thought I'd look around before I left."

Whatever happened next would determine whether she was going back to the maintenance office, out the front door, or home in a box.

"I'll just get on my way, then," she added, and started forward.

"Don't move," said Fischer, casually stepping in her direction. The sullen man remained near the bags. "Dan, here, made a call at my request. Turns out you don't work upstairs; neither does your imaginary friend Sheila."

There was Donovan's answer. Like it or not, she was about to be fighting for her life—again. She removed her faux glasses and put them safely in her purse, then unbuttoned her trench coat.

Donovan didn't scare easily, but there was something deadly about the setup: lots of concrete, steel, and bad intentions. One of these two men had killed thirty-five people that Donovan knew about: Daley Plaza, Charlie, Hannah, and Saul. And that was just in the past nine days. The sullen man wanted desperately to please the other. Neither would break a sweat ending Donovan's life in the solitude of the loading docks. Screaming would be pointless; cleanup would be easy. And if more loyal monsters were recruited to the basement—she would be dead.

Showtime.

"You know who I am?" she asked Fischer, placing her clutch and coat over a huge sealed drum next to a stack of orange caution cones.

"It finally came to me. You look somewhat different than you did on TV, but of course, I know who you are. You're the cunt who did her best to make sure Mason got convicted for killing those four niggers." He grinned and stepped closer in her direction. "Seems your best wasn't good enough, was it, bitch?"

That was exactly what she needed. Donovan no longer felt fear, just anticipation.

"Well, now, you are not one to be talking about anybody's best not being good enough, Dave. Seems you shot up a whole heap of folks just trying to kill little ol' me. That may actually make you the worst shot in the world. That might be Ripley's Believe It or Not shit, right there. I mean, how hard can it be?"

He pulled out a Glock from his jacket pocket. "I got half the job done. You just got lucky. You've been lucky for too goddamn long." He pointed the barrel of the gun at her head. "But your luck just ran out."

Donovan wondered what Dave Fischer meant by "getting half the job done." She also wondered how she was going to live another few minutes, stepping toward him as he pointed the gun.

"Hey," Dan hollered. Both Donovan and Dave turned, as the man hadn't spoken or moved since he and his higher up entered the loading docks. He had graduated from the bags to just in front of the compactor. "Dave, check this out. They finally got the new compactor, man ..." He hit a large green button on the machine and the mechanism started to whir. The noise resonated, bouncing off the concrete and metal surrounding it. He then waved his fingers in the air directly in front of a panel below the green button. Smiling, he said, "And I got the code." He punched in four numbers on the panel, and the metal door slowly rolled open.

Humored by his young associate's ingenuity, Dave Fischer dropped his firing arm a few inches and chuckled. "I like it, Dan. That's a great idea. I'll shoot the bitch and we can get her ground up before the blood hits the floor. Awesome." Both men clearly delighted with this fresh idea, Dave turned back to Donovan and again raised the Glock. "Time to take out the trash."

Donovan was now close enough to kick the gun from his hand—and did. He bared his teeth, about to lunge, but she lunged first, ramming her head into his midsection hard enough to knock him over. Now he was disoriented and pissed, a bad combination. In the second she had before he regrouped, she kicked him in the face. He passed out.

Sullen Dan came at her, fist doubled, but she had time to pick up the gun and had it aimed at him before he landed his punch. "Okay, Dan," she said as he puffed and glared. "Let's think this thing through. I believe you and Dave got into a disagreement. That's why he shot you."

The man bolted toward her like a horse from a starting gate. She shot him in the knee. He yelled as he hit the ground. "Stay still, Dan. I want to chat with you for a minute. Okay? We good, you and me?"

He barked. Not once, as she had heard from others in his dark fraternity, but he barked a number of times, like a neighbor's dog that just wouldn't quit. Eventually, he did. "All right, I'll take that as a yes," she said, squatting down so that they were face-to-face but not near enough that he could reach her. The blood from the bullet wound began to pool around him on the floor.

"What was the other part of Fischer's job that morning in Daley Plaza? Who else was he supposed to kill?"

Dan showed her his teeth. His breathing became labored and his face pinched.

"Dan—Dan, what's the answer?"

There was no response.

"Where's Mason Ghetz, Dan?"

The sullen man laughed a quiet, hissing sort of laugh as he held his leg. Donovan stood up. "Okay, one more thing. Alabama ..."

Surprised by the reference, he glanced up, and she shot him in the face. Behind her, Dave Fischer let out a small moan barely audible over the compactor. Donovan dropped the gun and turned. She casually stepped over to where he lay on the concrete, bent down, and pinched the side of his neck. Again, he was unconscious.

She had precious little time to get the body moved, but Donovan was motivated.

Dragging him to the compactor wasn't too hard. They weren't that far from it at that point. Getting him in an upright position proved to be difficult, but she persevered. Inching the dead weight up and over the lip of the metal bin took its toll. She ended up falling in with him. Once she got herself out of the box, she had a thought. That phone of his would have all kinds of information on it, she figured—certainly Bob Lynch's contact information, maybe even Mason Ghetz's.

Getting in the contraption without lugging a body turned out to be somewhat easier, and she was able to locate the phone in his pants and get back out just as he was coming out of his fog.

While catching her breath, she studied the control panel of the compactor and hit the "close" button. As slowly as it had opened, the metal door closed, sealing off the device and readying it for use. Now alert, Fischer reacted as she expected, banging on the metal door, yelling for her to open it, and shrieking.

Donovan leaned her tired arms against the machine, staring at a sign posted on the shiny red paint. "Hey, Dave," she said, "there are some rules we need to follow when using this compactor, okay?"

"Shut the fuck up, you fucking cunt! Open the fucking door!"

"Hey, now, you know what they say about honey and vinegar, Dave."

"I'm going to have your head on a fucking stick, you fucking cunt. You're going to wish you were dead. Do you hear me?"

"I hear you, Dave. But, Dave, you're locked in a trash compactor, okay? All right, this says we have to make sure all trash is securely bagged. I believe your ass has been securely bagged, so we're good."

His voice went hoarse from yelling. His insults turned to pleas.

"Next, comply with all recycling regulations. I don't think that applies to us. No batteries or oil, no furniture. Oh, the last one—no toxic materials. I can't think of anything more toxic than you, Dave. I feel a little bad breaking that one rule, but hey, as you well know, rules get broken all the time."

"Don't do this," he begged as she pulled the lever.

She remained until the screaming stopped.

Grabbing her trench coat and purse from atop the large plastic barrel, she took off for the maintenance office with Dave Fischer's phone in hand.

When she got there, Craig Apperson was still sitting at his desk. No longer pushing papers around, he sat slumped slightly forward, hands clasped in the prayer position, though he didn't seem to be praying. He appeared to be thinking, his eyes fixed straight ahead at nothing. That's what it looked like to Donovan, who once again observed the shift supervisor from the doorframe as she had less than an hour earlier, two killings ago.

She calculated this man's involvement. He would have been in charge of lining things up so that Dave Fischer had access to whatever he needed that night, and he knew that Charlie would be eliminated so that Fischer could take his place. He had cleared the way. He had covered the tracks.

Donovan rapped on the glass door. Craig Apperson leaped from his chair as if someone had just said, "Stick 'em up," and stared at Donovan with his mouth hanging open. Donovan snapped a picture of that reaction with Dave Fischer's phone.

"People are always so surprised to see me," she mused. "Ghetz had the same look on his face the first time we met."

Craig saw the flag sticker on the back of the phone. "How did you get Dave's phone?" he asked, frowning.

"Don't worry about it, Craig. Your pal doesn't need it anymore."

The man became unsteady, inching a few feet deeper into the room, and braced himself against the desk that held the coffee supplies.

Donovan put Fischer's cell in her clutch. "Listen, Craig, I'm counting on there being all sorts of information the police and I are going to want on that cell of Dave's, but you could save me a lot of precious time by answering just a couple tiny questions."

"Where's Dave?" Craig asked, his voice cracking nervously.

"Dave's dead. Dan's dead too. You know Dan?"

Craig pulled out a chair and sat down abruptly. Donovan thought how his responses were so different than those of Dan's or Dave's. This man seemed concerned.

"Were you thinking about what might be going on at the loading docks before I walked back in here just now? I mean, you knew Dave had talked to Dan and that the two of them were going to—meet me there, right? Were you thinking that they killed me?" she asked lightheartedly.

The man didn't speak, not out of insolence, but out of confusion and fear.

"Well, now you know how that turned out," she said, taking her own phone out of her purse and pulling up a picture of Bob Lynch. "Craig"—she stepped toward the chair he had flopped into—"you know this man?" She shoved the phone in his face. He did not respond.

"Look, Bubba, right now you're an accessory to murder. You are the bad man who helped the very bad man that night. You can get some serious time for a crime like that. On the other hand, if you answer the question, you and I never met. So ..." She pushed the photo in front of him again. "Where is Bob Lynch?"

When her heel made contact with his testicles, he went down, falling from the chair to his knees on the cheap industrial carpet beneath him. Donovan repeated the question.

"He's one of the supervisors," he gasped. "It's almost six. He's probably at the Brooks Building over on Jackson Boulevard. I'm not one of them. Don't kill me."

"I understood that Bob owned a chop shop. He's a maintenance supervisor?"

"Yeah," he managed through the pain. "I think he used to own some kind of auto repair. That's … all I know. Don't kill me," he directed her again.

"Thank you, Craig. Now, who else was Dave aiming to shoot when he took out all those people in Daley Plaza?"

The man stared at her blankly.

"Dave told me he took care of half of what he set out to do. Killing me and … who else?"

She could see the wheels turning in his rattled head. "Maurice?" he said, unsure.

Donovan remembered him. "Maurice Brown? The officer from the Bureau of Investigations?"

He shook his head affirmatively. "I think so."

Maurice Brown, the affable man she'd had coffee with that morning along with Jordan, the man standing next to her when the bodies started to fall, his among them.

"Why?" she asked.

"I don't know. Look, I swear to God, I don't know," he answered.

Donovan assessed that he was telling the truth. She would have to make sense of why Maurice was anybody's target when she had the leisure. Now was not the time.

"Okay, Craig, one more thing and I'll be on my way. There's a cleaning lady who works here named Beth Ann Washington. Do you know her?"

His breathing had become more regular. It appeared to Donovan that he was attempting to get up off the ground, so she kept that from happening. He yelled and curled in a fetal position. "No, no, I don't."

"Where do you keep the records of your employees?"

He gestured with his head to his desk. "Agh! There's … an icon on the desktop. Employees."

She stepped to the computer and found the file among fifty others cluttering the screen. "I have never understood why people leave so many icons on their computers. There is a place for everything, Craig. Cluttered surroundings mean a cluttered mind."

While reprimanding him, she ran through an extensive list of employees that was, thankfully, in alphabetical order. She jotted down Beth Ann's contact info on a Post-It and stuck it in her purse. When things settled down, she intended to get in touch with Beth Ann. In a big city like Chicago, Donovan was certain she could find the lady better employment, something with benefits, something—less dangerous. She stepped away from the man who was either still unable to get up or unwilling to try. "Thank you, Craig. You've been very helpful."

She left the office and started down the hall, then stopped. Leaning against the wall, she reflected. "Sloppy," she said, and returned to the office, closing the door behind her.

Chapter Nineteen

Stepping over the body, Donovan pulled the faux glasses from her purse and, once again, slid them on. She turned off the lights and locked the office door on the way out. Finding the freight elevator that brought her down to sub-basement two, she rode it all the way to the lobby without company. The freight elevator allowed her to avoid any unnecessary human interaction on her way out of the Chicago Temple Building.

She made eye contact with no one, straight through the lobby leading to the exit. The guard she had signed in with was busy helping someone else, and the smattering of other people coming or going were caught up in their own endeavors, much to Donovan's liking. She moved at an even, relaxed pace. No one paid any attention to her. No one knew about the two bodies in the loading docks and another in the maintenance office.

But she knew.

Hitting the pavement, city lights up and down Washington Street tripped on as twilight waned. She didn't glance back at the famous building that currently held her little secret. She felt satisfied knowing that Chicago was a little safer now that the man who had pulled the trigger on Daley Plaza was the size of a professionally packaged laundry bundle. "You're welcome," she said aloud in the InterPark parking lot as she climbed behind the wheel of her car.

Eight minutes, maybe ten would get her to the Brooks Building on the corner of Jackson and Franklin where, if Craig Apperson was correct, she would finally have the opportunity to meet Bob Lynch. *Don't let me down, Bob,* she thought. *You are my very best shot at finding him tonight. And it needs to be tonight. For a free man, Mr. Ghetz has turned out to be one elusive motherfucking butterfly.*

She took out her cell and opened a Parkopedia app to determine the closest parking for the building. Thirteen dollars would buy her two hours in the lot on South Wells, which would mean an approximately two-minute walk to her destination. Close enough to be convenient and far enough away to keep a low profile should anyone be watching her come or go, the lot Donovan rolled into was perfect; she turned off the ignition.

Taking a moment to pull down the visor and flip on the overhead light in the Prius, she checked her appearance in the mirror, ready for her next performance as Jessica Tucker. Exiting the car, she took off on foot toward West Jackson. The temperature seemed to be dipping from the low sixties to the low forties as she walked. That was not atypical for October in the Windy City, and invigorating to the woman who could still smell the cheap aftershave worn by her most recent victim.

The Brooks Building, another Chicago landmark, stood directly across the street. Donovan had always admired the building: beautiful, resilient, clean lines, and always well-manicured. She slowed to take it in and assess the surroundings. The old Chicago school–type architecture of the structure had been open to the public since 1910, and its intended impact had valiantly stood the test of time.

A twelve-story high-rise located in the heart of the city's commercial district, the terra-cotta masonry covering its steel frame remained intact.

Detailed carvings along the top of the top floor appeared unscathed by more than a century of rough Chicago weather, and the busy shops and eateries around the building's periphery threw off a charming, friendly glow of inside lights and outside signage that made the neighborhood inviting.

Next to the alley, Donovan located the glass doors leading into the lobby. "Brooks Building" was etched in the stone above. She made her way across the polished black linoleum past two elevators on her right and directly to the check-in desk next to a stairwell banistered with black wrought iron fashioned in another century.

The desk was attended by a middle-aged woman busy readying herself to leave for the day. While buttoning her parka and wrapping a thick wool scarf around her neck, she said, "May I help you? I was just about to leave. Gotta catch the L."

"Sorry. I won't take a second. I'm looking for Bob Lynch, the maintenance supervisor. He's expecting me. I'm Jessica Tucker. I'm here to see him about a new building contract he is going to be taking on. He asked me to swing it by." The doctor smiled warmly while adjusting her glasses.

"Okay, let's see if I can find him. He moves around a lot." The woman made a call. No one answered. She called another number, her anxiety at needing to leave apparent on her face. No one answered at that number either.

"He's not answering the office number or his cell. Look, usually, we do a whole check-in thing, but I gotta go. Just sign this." She pointed to a clipboard holding a sign-in sheet on the counter. "I'm not gonna worry about your ID. You look trustworthy to me." She smiled. So did Donovan, but for different reasons.

Fighting with the zipper of her parka, she continued, "He might be on twelve. There's an office space up there where the maintenance folks used to hang out to eat, leave their coats while they're working, stuff like that. They've got a real break room down here now, but a lot of the crew prefer the old space because it's deserted up there right now. You're welcome to check it out if you like. The elevators are right there and, well"—she smiled, pointing out the obvious—"the stairs are right here. I am sorry, but I gotta go. Running late." And with that the woman was out the door, leaving Donovan alone at the desk.

Donovan returned to the elevators, pushed a button, and waited. After she entered, two people rushed to catch it with her but, fortunately, they didn't make it. She was on her own and headed for the twelfth floor. Donovan couldn't believe her luck. She had cornered Bob Lynch at last.

When the elevator door opened on the twelfth floor, Donovan could feel her heart pumping. Little provoked that kind of physical response in the doctor, but Ghetz and everything wrapped around him inspired an atypical reaction from her.

The halls were relatively empty. A man buttoning his coat and clutching a stack of real estate flyers in one hand got on the elevator that she had just stepped out of, and two maintenance workers wearing uniformed jumpsuits were walking in her direction toward that same elevator, though they would have to wait for the next one to arrive.

As they got close enough for Donovan to speak to them conversationally, she smiled and asked if they knew where she could find Bob Lynch, explaining that the front desk receptionist thought he might be on that floor. The two glanced at one another, clearly not sure what the answer was. The taller of the two said, "Uh, maybe he's hanging out in the old break room."

The shorter one added, "Yeah, I haven't seen him around. We just came up here to check the bathrooms. Most of maintenance is down in the rest of the building cleaning the offices. They just renovated this floor, so the suites are all empty right now. They're getting them rented out, though, I think."

The elevator door opened, and as the two got in, the taller man stuck his foot in the metal frame to activate the sensor and keep it from closing. "It's not really a break room. It was, but they moved the break room to the first floor. Now this one is usually empty. But people still take breaks there sometimes, and the door is usually open."

The shorter worker regarded the taller one. "I think that's where they talk to the real estate people about renting out the spaces. I think there's still a table in there."

The taller nodded at his coworker, then turned back to Donovan.

"If you want to check it out, it's all the way down this hall and to your right just a little past the supply closet, same side of the hall. If he's not there, try the real break room on the first floor."

Donovan thanked them as the man allowed the metal door to shut.

A quietness in the air suggested that no one else was around. As Donovan cautiously walked the length of the long hall, she observed that what the young man had told her appeared to be accurate. She saw no company names attached to any of the offices that she passed.

Turning right at the end of the corridor, she passed the supply closet the young man had mentioned and a ladies' room followed by a men's. Only a few steps farther, she could hear people talking and stopped to assess their location. She didn't want Bob Lynch walking out of a room and finding her in the hall. If he was up there, Donovan intended to be the surprise, not the other way around. Standing still, she could make out two men having a conversation. She took two more steps and stopped again.

"Can I have some of that coffee?" one man asked the other.

"Knock yourself out. It's been there since this morning," said the other.

She took another step toward the open door, which appeared to be pulled all the way back. Because the door provided no cover, she could not step any closer for fear of being seen.

Neither man spoke while coffee was poured. Donovan could hear a string of other noises. This was a prime opportunity for her to test her skills at the profiling game she played in the parking lot of the Pretty Baby Hair and Nails.

Lid hitting a glass pot after the coffee was poured. Not a fancy machine. Mr. Coffee or the like. Poured into a paper cup, not a mug. Thin metal scuffling slightly on concrete. They're sitting in folding chairs on a bare floor. The slight echo suggests a lack of furniture or anything that would muffle sound. This is an unincorporated space. Not ready to be rented, waiting to be finished.

Now, she had to be patient to find out if she had won the game. She always won the game. While the one man slurped the stale coffee, the other spoke.

"I just don't like you coming here. Too fucking public. I thought we agreed that you need to stay underground for a little while, at least until the news stops covering all this shit."

"We need to talk."

"So use your fucking phone. I ... I could go sit in your car and we can talk. This isn't cool."

"That dinner the other night was fucked up. Donna was all weird. That attorney is like a fucking actress or some shit. Who talks like that?"

Donovan heard someone stepping across the concrete and then a window being pushed open. One of the men struck a match and slowly exhaled.

"I thought it would look better for us to have the boys over, try to make some kind of party out of it. They all pitched in. I called in a lot of fucking favors, dude. As far as my cunt wife goes, she's weird as a way of life. She doesn't give a shit about you, man. You take everything so fucking ... personal. And we don't need to see that attorney again, I fucking hope to God. Is this really what you needed to talk about, Mason?"

"No. We need to talk about a couple other more pressing situations."

Donovan leaned her head against the nearest wall, smiling ear to ear, her head tilted toward the ceiling. She hadn't only found Bob Lynch, she had found Bob Lynch and his lover, Mason Ghetz. *One-stop shopping,* she mused, knowing exactly what would happen next. How it happened was the only question remaining.

Bob Lynch exhaled again, then closed the window and returned to the table. She heard the familiar sound of a pill bottle being opened, capsules tapping against one another on their way out. The lid was reapplied, followed by a slurp of coffee.

"No thanks. Yeah, maybe. What the fuck? Hey, seriously, don't come here again. I don't need any shit. This landlord ain't one of us."

Again, the bottle opened and closed, followed by the chair being pushed back out and a second cup of coffee being poured.

"Here. Take this." Passing off the paper cup, Ghetz reseated himself across from Lynch. "I'm free, Bob. Hey, look at me—I'm free, okay? It's all good. If somebody walks in, which they won't, we ain't doing anything illegal. Now, stop whining like the fucking fag you are and listen to me. We have to sort some shit out."

Lynch chuckled softly. "Well, everybody's gone now, so I guess this is as good a place as any. What's the problem?"

"Okay, there's three things needing attention. First, I can't move shit since Daryl got himself killed. That club was my bread and butter. I sure as fuck can't use it anymore. Cops crawling up and down the walls like cockroaches."

"Do it like you used to. Do it on the street. Just wait a couple of weeks. Are you telling me you need money?"

"Goddamn it, Bob, I ain't asking for money."

"That's good. Between that Dean bitch and the other one and those two pieces of shit on the jury, I'm a little strapped myself, partner."

"Yeah, I know. Jesus Christ, you want me to tell you how grateful I am again?"

"Shut up."

"Want me to suck you off right here in the Brooks Building?"

"I said shut the fuck up, Mason." A growl entered Lynch's voice, making him sound like loose gravel under heavy boots.

"I need another club, one like the Satin Door. I was thinking maybe I could start building up some business at that one over on—"

"No. You're not dealing anything until this shit settles. Fuck, Mason!"

Lynch's chair moved away from the desk or table he was sitting at, but Donovan did not hear him rise. After deciding that there was no need to run for cover, she continued listening to this intimate conversation the way her grandmother had listened to radio shows, the way millennials listened to podcasts.

"Okay, okay, whatever. The other thing is, what are we doing about Maurice?" Ghetz asked.

"What about him?" Lynch countered.

"Well, what if they link him to the other shit? What if they find out he was working for the AB?"

Donovan stood rapt. Maurice Brown, a black man employed by Special Investigation for the State was working for the Aryan Brotherhood? That didn't make sense to her.

"How would they find out? And what the fuck if they did?" Lynch finally posed after considering the question.

Ghetz quickly jumped in over Lynch's curt response.

"Look, I get why you and the higher-ups wanted to take him out. I get it. He was getting soft. He'd served his purpose. But now there's a hole, right? Nothing is moving, no money, no dope, nothing. Who we got on the inside to move anything right now? Who we got that's gonna look the other way? And Bob, somebody's gonna tie this shit together: Daley Plaza, Maurice, my ass. And when they do, they are gonna be up on that shit like white on rice. Me walking pissed off all of those sonsofbitches. They ain't gonna let it happen twice. And when it comes down, a whole buttload of us are going down with it, not just me."

Silence filled the room, followed by feet shuffling under a table. Clearly, Ghetz had given Lynch much to think through. After concluding that any answers to the big questions would have to come later, Lynch responded.

"That's not going to happen, Mason. Jesus fucking Christ, you're like an old woman, for fuck sake. Just cool it. The Maurice thing will get taken care of. Just chill the fuck out. This is Chicago, dude. We own this shit."

Ghetz let out an exasperated sigh. "Yeah. Yeah, okay. But there's one more thing."

"You are one exhausting motherfucker. Have I ever told you that?"

"That nigger—that nigger who said all that shit about me. I want her dead, Bob. I want her dead. I want it to be slow. I want to hear her beg, and I want it done by *my* hand."

Lynch apparently liked that list of aspirations.

"Who's stopping you?" He chuckled.

The conversation then dissolved into something much less weighty covering inane banter about the media's desire to get interviews with Ghetz and the rowdy get-together Lynch had thrown in his friend's honor the night after his acquittal. They shared a laugh over one of their "brothers" who had, the week before, gotten himself stuck in an air duct while trying to spy on his ex-wife and her new boyfriend.

Even the fleas have fleas, Donovan thought.

The doctor had heard enough, and if she was going to leverage having found both of them into a two-for-the-price-of-one opportunity, her timing would be crucial.

Working the black leather gloves around her fingers to make sure they were on as tightly as possible, she hurried to the ladies' room next to the supply closet and ducked inside, quickly removing the nose bridge and glasses but leaving her hair pulled back. She secured the bathroom door open with a kick stop and fished around her big clutch for Dave Fischer's cell phone. Then she unzipped a small pouch inside the purse where she always kept a burner phone in working order.

It wasn't hard finding Bob Lynch's number on Dave Fischer's phone. He had him in his "favorites" list. From inside the bathroom, Donovan pulled up the number and keyed it into her burner. It only took one ring before connecting to the next white supremacist she would be killing that evening.

"Yeah?" Lynch asked.

Thinly veiling her voice by modulating it a notch higher than normal, Donovan said, "Mr. Lynch, I'm sorry to call you on your cell, but this is urgent and you weren't in the office, so … Anyway, you need to get down here right away. There are two cops at the desk asking for you. They say they have a search warrant."

"A search warrant?" he asked incredulously.

"I am sorry. I'm supposed to leave, Mr. Lynch, but I'll stay here until you get down to the desk. I don't know what it's about. They won't say."

Donovan hung up.

"Hello?" Lynch said, then realizing she had hung up, he stared at the phone as if it might explain what was going on.

"What's that about?" Mason asked.

"Who the fuck knows. Two pigs with a search warrant downstairs."

"A search warrant for what?"

"Who the fuck knows? Stay here. I'll be right back."

He thought about the woman who worked at the front desk of the Brooks Building. Whoever called sounded nothing like her, and no one sat at the desk in the evening. Lynch considered what might actually be going on as he hurried down the hall on his way to the elevator. If the cops were there, whether the call had been staged or not, he needed to check it out.

But when he passed the ladies' room, Donovan greeted him with a whack on the head, using the metal lid of the trash can stationed inside. He went down without a peep. He didn't even see it coming.

She fished around in his pockets until she located the building's master key ring. Leaving him for a moment, she went to the nearby supply closet, trying each of the keys until the door opened. The storage space held shelves lined with cleaning products and stacks of towels. *This will do nicely*, she thought, spotting industrial-sized jugs of bleach and ammonia on the floor. Combining even a small amount of those two common cleaning products would create a toxic chlorine gas. And the amount at her disposal would be deadly. *How poetic*.

Adrenaline had always been Donovan's friend, and dragging Bob Lynch from the hall to inside the supply closet did not prove to be a difficult task. Once she had him pulled to the back as far as possible, she moved the ammonia and bleach to the front near the door and gathered an armful of crisp white towels from an unsealed parcel. If her plans went as she intended, she would need those towels in mere minutes. Placing them just outside the small room in the hall, she turned to readdress the man on the floor.

Lynch had started to shake off the fog of unconsciousness brought on by the blow to his head. She knelt next to him, jostling his shoulders until he rose on one elbow. With his head now off the tile, it was easier for her to knock him out again with a hard punch to the nose. Donovan wasn't fond of this move. Punches were effective but impacted her knuckles. Nevertheless, it worked.

She extracted the cell phone from his pants to locate Ghetz's number. "So many phones," she muttered, swiping it open. Ghetz was on Lynch's speed dial. "Let's you and me get all caught up, Mason," she whispered into the dank air of the small chamber.

Before touching the icon for Ghetz, she peered at Bob Lynch splayed out near the toilet paper and paper towels. "Damn it, Bob, you are going to be conscious again in another few seconds, and it's going to fall upon me to deal with that."

Placing his cell phone on the shelf closest to her hand, she considered the options available. Untying two bundles of towels, she brought both lengths of twine as well as a small blue rag to Lynch's limp body. Wrapping twice around his ankles with one piece of twine and three times around his wrists with the other, she felt better about the situation. Neither end of him had been tied all that well so that Ghetz could easily extract the thick string when he joined his partner. Then she stuffed the blue rag into Lynch's partially open mouth.

"Think of this as a kind of ball gag, Bob," she said softly while working in the corners of the cloth. "Maybe that will make this more enjoyable for you. I don't know if you like that sort of thing, but like it or not, you *are* about to get fucked."

She got up and grabbed the phone from the shelf, this time calling Mason Ghetz.

"What's up?" he asked upon answering. "What do they want?"

Ghetz was still under the impression that Lynch was dealing with police in the lobby.

"*Hellooo*, Mr. Ghetz. Remember me?" Donovan cooed into the cell.

Momentary silence on the other end suggested he did not, not right away. Donovan could feel the rusted wheels in his brain spinning as he frantically tried to place the voice.

"You are a sneaky, wicked little elf, you know that? It's been quite an adventure finding you—a big, wonderful adventure."

"Who the fuck is this? Where's Bob?"

"I just want you to know that I agree with your boyfriend. If you want to kill me—who's stopping you?"

White nationalist, neo-Nazi, and proud member of the Aryan Brotherhood, Mason Ghetz leaped to his feet so fast that the folding chair he had been sitting on toppled onto its side. A thin stream of urine made its way down the left pant leg of his jeans.

"Where's Bob?" he shouted into the phone.

During their conversation, Donovan had unscrewed the bleach and ammonia and begun pouring out the contents onto the tile beneath her. Careful to not get any on her clothes and boots, she emptied one and then the other as fumes began to envelop the space.

"Just like you," she said to Ghetz, "he's in the closet."

Mason Ghetz rubbed one eye with his palm. "Bitch, where are you?" he yelled again.

"That doesn't matter, Mason. But Bob is in a bit of a jam."

"I'm going to have your head on a stick, you filthy cunt. Let me talk to Bob!"

"You are *delightful*. He's in the supply closet just down the hall."

She ended the call and placed the phone back in Lynch's pocket. The fumes had gotten bad fast, and she had to cover her mouth and nose with another towel. After resealing the jugs and pushing them into a corner, she hid behind the open door, counting on Mason Ghetz to hurry.

Bob Lynch became alert before Ghetz arrived. That allowed him a moment to fully grasp his predicament: he was bound and gagged, noxious chemicals were filling his nostrils, and Donovan Montgomery was standing behind the door, her eyes smiling at him from above the towel that covered most of her face.

Ghetz did exactly what she hoped he would. Upon seeing Bob on the floor, he dove to his knees to untie him despite Bob's pantomimed urging for him to check behind the door. But the signal was not understood. And before Ghetz had removed the rag from Lynch's mouth, Donovan stepped out of the room and locked the door.

Her prey secured, she braced herself against the wall, gasping in fresh oxygen. As Donovan regrouped, a vaguely disoriented Ghetz and now terrified Lynch banged against the closet door, slinging insults and making threats. But the chlorine gas that the bleach and ammonia had created was quickly getting the better of them both.

Donovan then tucked the white towels she had placed in the hall under the door from the outside to keep the gas from escaping. "You say you want to kill me," she said loudly enough for them to hear over their rage. "You want it to be slow. You want to hear me beg, and you want it done by your own hand. Well, Mason Ghetz, this here is commonly referred to as—*karma*."

She leaned on the door, pressing herself against it: her gloved hands, her head, her shoulders and back. She knew what was happening inside the supply closet. As the men pounded and pleaded, swore and coughed, she knew that the gas had already burned out their eyes and that their lungs were struggling to function. Both men's breathing had been replaced by worthless gasps. She knew that their heart muscles pumped erratically now and that the chest pain had become unbearable. She knew that each man was calculating whether he would ever be leaving that closet or if he was going to die in there. And she knew the answer to that.

An expression of bliss spread across her pretty face as she slowly rolled over, opening her palms and pressing the front of her body against the door, thighs pulsing in time with the buckling wood as the two pounded and screamed. She wanted to mentally record their panic forever.

Closing her eyes, she relished each time they threw their weakening bodies at the locked exit. And every time one of them choked or let out a small sob, a warmth washed over her, her belly tingling with pleasurable sensations. She rubbed her moist cheek against the cheap paint, cherishing every plea for help until, finally, the gasps and gags, pounding and pleading ceased.

She remained until it was silent. She remained until she regained her composure. And when she could squeeze no more from the experience, she unlocked the door. There they were, Bob Lynch and Mason Ghetz, dead at her feet. She put the keys back in Lynch's pocket. *Let someone else figure this one out*, she thought, pushing the elevator button.

The McDonald's at the base of the Brooks Building looked inviting as she hit the street. Donovan was hungry but knew she would be pushing her good fortune to walk in and order something to eat. What if she was recognized? After all the good work she had done that day, it wasn't worth taking the chance. So, she took off for the parking lot on Wells.

While walking, she dialed the police. Masking her voice, she left a brief, anonymous tip that she hoped would guide them to finding out more than she had concerning Maurice Brown's involvement with the Aryan Brotherhood. She also gave them a few details tying Ghetz to the mass shooting vis-à-vis Bob Lynch.

She finished the call outside her car. Once inside, she snapped the burner in half and, using a nail file, destroyed the unit as she had done a dozen times with other disposable phones. She would get rid of the broken pieces later and place a new one inside the tiny zippered pouch. For the time being, she put the broken bits in a coat pocket and turned on the ignition.

Hitting one button for the heater and another for the radio, Donovan smiled. "Kudos, girl. You just gassed two Nazis," she said as "Living in Danger" by Ace of Base bounced around her front seat, keeping her company on the drive home.

Epilogue

The following day, a maintenance worker found the bodies of Mason Ghetz and Bob Lynch in the supply closet on the twelfth floor of the Brooks Building. The discovery rained down on Chicago like New Year's Eve confetti blanketing the city, unavoidable and impossible to ignore.

Each piece of information regarding the double murder proved to be more colorful than the last, making it a bumper day for the media. A white nationalist rally scheduled for that day was canceled while would-be participants tried to decipher what had actually happened to two of their own, and whether the stories circulating were true.

Donovan slept in.

On a bench at the corner of Michigan Avenue and Randolph Street, in a picturesque tree-lined area of Millennium Park, Jordan Payne and Donovan Montgomery clutched coffee cups, enjoying the smell and warming themselves on the steam. They were directly to the side of the Millennium Monument, a forty-foot-high semicircle of columns designed to replicate the original peristyle built in that very spot in the early 1900s. Impressive in its grace and grandeur, the two stared on admiringly between sips.

"It's damn hard to believe that Maurice Brown was the other person Dave Fischer had been hired to kill that morning. Maurice Brown. Special Investigations. A black man working for the Aryan Brotherhood. Shit." Jordan turned to face Donovan. "Apparently, before he worked for Special Investigations, he was a corrections officer. That's how he met Ghetz and Lynch. They started grooming him back then, having him move stuff in and out in exchange for money that their buddies in the Brotherhood would take care of on the outside. Unbelievable."

"Yeah," the doctor added. "Sometimes it's hard to know the good guys from the bad."

"Maurice must have been eaten up inside, stuck in a very difficult situation with no way out." Jordan drank the rest of his coffee, moved by the situation.

"That old saying is true, Counselor. When you make a deal with the devil, there's always hell to pay."

He shot her an expression of astonishment that dissolved quickly into sad resolve. "Man, Fischer had you right in the kill zone that morning. Too close."

"Well," she said, "I'm still here."

Jordan laughed lightly. "Yeah, it's gonna take more than a few Nazis to slow your roll, Doctor Montgomery."

"Damn straight."

"Those fools don't know who they're dealing with."

"Well"—she grinned—"a few of them do."

Jordan and Donovan watched as a stray dog leaped onto the base of the imposing work of art in front of them. The mutt relieved himself and sauntered off.

"Don't ever want to get too big for my britches, though," the doctor noted. "No matter how magnificent the work, there's always somebody ready and able to piss all over it."

They shared a laugh as Jordan gestured to her cup. "You done?" She handed the cardboard container to him as he got up to throw them away.

"I'll bet DuMont is delighted with how this business shook out."

Donovan nodded affirmatively. "He called yesterday after the autopsies came back confirming chloramine gas killed them both. I think he's happy to be done with it. Though they have confirmed it was murder, there's such a long list of people who wanted them both dead that he told me he isn't going to break a sweat over finding out who it was."

"Yeah, I get that. Hard to imagine over the past week, but there is other stuff going on in Chicago. He has a perpetually full plate, I'm sure."

Donovan paused, reflecting on the man who had basically given her a pass on a crime he was convinced she had committed. "He's a good man," she added.

Payne turned a bit more serious and added, "Ironic that Chicago isn't a death penalty state, and yet those two ended up getting the gas chamber. Hey, Nazis in the gas chamber!"

"Poetic," seconded Donovan. "Say, that election is just around the corner, mister. How do you think Jen is going to fare in the aftermath of Ghetz's demise?"

Jordan swiveled his head from side to side, smiling broadly. "Oh, yeah, she's a shoo-in now, baby. Every poll taken over the past two days is in her favor. I think the Brotherhood would have put up a stink and made things even worse, but the fact that Ghetz and Lynch had been lovers for so long threw a wrench in their collective position on the matter. Donna

Lynch was so eager to tell the cops all about Bob and Mason. Makes you think she'd been waiting to throw Bob under the bus for a long time." He looked squarely at Donovan. "Amazing timing, the police getting that anonymous tip. I mean, that's what got them looking closer at Maurice's MO and pinning the whole case together." He waited for her to speak. She did not. "You know anything about that, Doctor?"

Donovan met Jordan's eyes, admiring his polish and integrity. But she had no intention of dragging him into the truth. "You know," she said, "I've become terribly popular again."

"Is that right?"

"Mm-hmm. Seems now that everything I said on the stand has been confirmed, I have been forgiven by the masses."

"Well, go sell some books."

"Yes, sir, I think I will." She got up.

"You going into the office, Doctor?"

"No, I think I'm going to go shopping today. I need a new dress for tonight."

From the bench where he was still seated, Jordan fought against frowning at that. "Really, a new dress. Got big plans for tonight, do you?"

His attempt at nonchalance charmed Donovan. "Yeah, I have a date. He's taking me to BLVD, that swanky dinner house over on West Lake Street. You heard of it?"

Jordan's face fell. He nodded, managing a thin smile.

"Perfect. Pick me up at eight?"

It took him several seconds to figure out what she had said—and meant. Then he stood up, straightening his coat and showing all of his teeth.

"Eight it is."